T0129482

WIVES ON LAYAWAY

WIVES ON LAYAWAY

BAD BUSINESS

JOSEPH UBO

iUniverse

WIVES ON LAYAWAY
BAD BUSINESS

iUniverse books may be ordered through booksellers or by contacting:

iUniverse
1663 Liberty Drive
Bloomington, IN 47403
www.iuniverse.com
1-800-Authors (1-800-288-4677)

ISBN: 978-1-5320-0384-4 (sc)
ISBN: 978-1-5320-0383-7 (e)

Library of Congress Control Number: 2016912709

Print information available on the last page.

iUniverse rev. date: 06/02/2017

CHAPTER 1

EMMANUEL AWAK-ISANG DECIDED that his wife, Rose, needed to die. The choice was simple for him. Such decisions are always easy when a person feels terribly wronged. But carrying out a homicide without leaving a trail usually proves trickier than investing in a murder weapon. And that is just one obstacle.

As marriage counselors say, communication is the key to a relationship—perhaps even a bad one. Emmanuel did not clearly signal his intent to kill her, because of that omission, his wife kept messing up his plan. For one thing, she always had their twin babies with her. Though he believed he had been more wronged than any man in history, Emmanuel considered himself an ethical guy, and he did not want to leave bullet holes in his children or even splash blood on them while removing their mom from the land of the living.

But unlike a lot of people whose utterances, facial expressions, and body language show that they have had it with marriage, Emmanuel did not consider seeking relief via the tried-and-true American means: divorce. He was too full of ire to take that route. Emmanuel wanted to escape a relationship he considered to be a bad deal and to avoid any additional financial cost. He knew that because Texas was a community-property state, it would take a miracle to pull off

1

a divorce without losing his shirt. His blood pressure spiked at the thought that his wife would become a rich woman after their divorce. That's why he contemplated hiring an assassin to eliminate her. But in casual conversations with people who bragged that they knew people involved in such work, Emmanuel learned that most so-called contract killers were either outright frauds or wannabe police informers looking to clean their slates by luring others into crime.

Emmanuel wished for something familiar and simpler: dark magic, the much-talked-about African method of removing an enemy without firing an incriminating shot. But he recalled a warning that African voodoo loses its power to do deathly harm the moment it is transported overseas. That meant it would be a waste of money to import voodoo to America, where everything operates according to solid scientific facts, not by magic. He convinced himself that there had to be a necromancer in America who specialized in using magical powers to kill people like the sorcerers did in Africa. Emmanuel began by checking out fortune tellers and palm readers. Not only was contract killing not their specialty, but they did not know anyone who could carry out a hit without a physical agent such as poison or a hunting rifle or a ploy like an arranged accident. They were no help. He searched more discreetly without asking the advice of friends.

Under the pretext of attending out-of-town job fairs, Emmanuel traveled to Louisiana, Arkansas, and Mississippi. But even in the seediest areas of those states, he could not find voodoo priests willing to see to the accidental death of his wife. He was losing time and had no help in sight. In desperation, he decided to do the deed himself as he had initially planned. He borrowed a textbook on anatomy and physiology from the public library. Since he had used family connections to skip biology and other required science courses in high school, he did not know much about the workings of the human body. Thank goodness for the resources of American libraries.

Emmanuel immersed himself in colorful biology tomes. They helped him to identify the exact locations of vital blood vessels where one stab would end the life of a useless woman in no time. Having found in those library books the life-supplying conduits to a beating heart, he purchased a chemical suit, safety goggles, and two daggers. Whenever Rose was out of the house and he was alone, Emmanuel stood in front of mirrors and practiced how he would stab the life out of her without getting her evil blood on him. He also ordered old copies of the British magazine *True Detective* and studied them day and night, as if preparing for an entrance examination at Eton, the expensive boarding school in England.

But after also watching many hours of news and crime shows on American television and noticing the ease with which law enforcement personnel connected the dots following a homicide, Emmanuel reconsidered his plan for a do-it-yourself murder. He was amazed at how adept the American police were in linking homicides to husbands who had taken out hefty life insurance policies on their wives, as he had.

Though the efficiency of US law enforcement caused him anxiety and gave him second thoughts, Emmanuel made a small investment in a handgun called a Saturday-night special and had it fitted with a silencer. After practicing the effective operation of the gun in front of the full-length mirror in his bedroom, he was impressed with American ingenuity in designing what he referred to as a "settler of disputes." Using the gun did not require much work or special training. He laughed at his foolishness in considering any other means of committing the murder.

Not long before, Emmanuel had booby-trapped his wife's car. But he had to undo his work in a hurry after Rose decided to take their twins to day care. After that near-miss with his babies, he settled on shooting their mom from a distance to make it look like someone else did it. But that plan also hit a snag. The twins took ill on the day he had chosen to hide behind the chimney on the roof of his town house and shoot Rose as she was pulling into the driveway. On that day the babies could not be separated from their mom.

But this is getting ahead of the story. Let us back up a little.

Emmanuel's problems with his wife were rooted in events that had taken place more than ten years earlier. He had returned home to marry, and his family introduced him to several girls who were raised in and around the community where he'd grown up. These were girls whose histories and pedigrees his people knew quite well. They discreetly showcased these girls for him, but none was his type. The family did not know that he was looking for an extremely light-skinned girl, the kind he saw in fashion magazines displayed at the checkout counters in American convenience stores. Emmanuel was angling for a local babe who would be the envy of his friends back in the States. He also wanted a graduate of a midwife school who could become a registered nurse in America.

The girls who were scouted out and brought to him for show-and-tell, though excellent material for building strong marriages and good homes did not remotely look like the beauty queens he saw in fashion magazines and on American college campuses.

Emmanuel conned his family, which, like many in Africa, insisted on being front and center when the children had the itch to get hitched. He told his people that with his high level of education and his exposure to other cultures, he was not a candidate for an arranged marriage. He shocked his family by saying that he wanted a marriage based on love, not an arbitrary pairing by people who valued domesticity far more than beauty.

Though his people did not say so, they suspected that Emmanuel had immoral intentions. In their view, any young man who did not want his family telling him whom to choose for a wife must have something to hide. They thought he wanted to do his own scouting so he could sample the girls with devil-may-care attitudes, the ones who, to the consternation of their parents, had outgrown the boundaries set by their elders and by the culture.

Emmanuel visited a lot of college campuses in his quest for a likely beauty-pageant winner. A few of the girls, mostly members of a Puritan-influenced sect that billed itself as the Evangelicals of the Church for West Africans, noticed him everywhere they turned and decided he was up to no good. When they saw him at their scripture study meetings without the required King James Version Study Bible, they got suspicious. They told each other that to finish the race set before them and to receive the crown of life from the Lord for living piously on a rowdy, party-oriented university campus, they needed to avoid the man with the shiny Mercedes-Benz as they would the devil incarnate. So despite the hard currency Emmanuel displayed at the campus exchange, these girls, who prided themselves on being good role models and on being seen as wholesome, were not impressed.

It just so happened that while Emmanuel was working the party circuit and the prayer meetings of born-again, Holy Ghost–baptized girls, several girls were in the final stages of assembling a band christened the Virgins. The band's main purpose was to offer a flesh-and-blood example of moral rectitude to younger girls who might have thought that there was no oasis from the encroaching wilderness of materialism. The band girls refused to be charmed by what they called the "vanity of ostentation," which they knew Emmanuel to personify. They encouraged other girls to focus on their studies and not to allow themselves to be victimized by the latest ravishing wolf on campus. Other girls on campus heard about the heroics of the scripture girls and began to show courage, refusing the enticement to be playthings for the man wearing expensive suits and driving gleaming cars. The boycott was so effective that the swaggering Emmanuel noticed that most girls went in the opposite direction when they spotted him in their residence halls. But since he thought so highly of himself, he believed this meant that all girls who resisted him were what King James calls maidens. He hurriedly promised marriage to a girl who was not nearly as puritanical as the band sisters.

Unlike the Virgin-band girls, the one Emmanuel chose strutted around campus in stilettos, low-cut blouses, and hot shorts instead of the required sandals and full-length dresses.

Since Rose could neither read sheet music nor played any musical instrument, she was regarded only as an associate of the band girls. They knew she attended their meetings solely to con heaven into improving her luck in finding a rich man to take care of her, so they did not insist that she conform to their standards and their dress code.

Shortly after his marriage proposal to a girl everyone thought he hardly knew, Emmanuel returned to America. But before he flew out, he saddled his family with the responsibility of getting her over to the United States through a visa program for wives joining husbands. The complete paperwork for that class of visa was on file before he left, but unknown to him, the girl and the busiest US embassy in Africa did not get along well. Rose and the office staff were not on speaking terms. Emmanuel's older family members interceded but could not get the embassy or the girl to tell them why the mention of her name generated a negative response at the embassy. They gave up. Emmanuel's younger cousins, who saw nothing wrong with their American cousin marrying a girl they may have dallied with in the immediate past, made a concerted effort but found no one at the embassy who would take a bribe and tell them what was in her record and, more important, how to make it disappear. They too gave up.

Emmanuel sent them an aerogram demanding to know why it was taking them so long to get his girl to him. The cousins went to the head office of the Nigeria Telecommunications Corporation in Lagos and placed a call to him on a secure line. They told him Rose was too much trouble. They pleaded with him to heed the admonitions of the family elders and to leave her behind. The cousins also asked him to permit them to find another girl and to put her on layaway for him. Emmanuel did not want to hear that. He said he was deeply in love with the girl he had found himself. They said it was impossible for a real man to be that badly smitten in such a short time. He said he resented being told that he was less than a man and vowed not to abandon his dream girl.

The cousins reported back to the elders in the village, and the entire family washed its hands off the situation. Having ended communication with family members, Emmanuel consulted with Africans in the United States about his problem. They too told him that he should look for another girl and that they believed the spirits of his ancestors were trying to help him avoid a catastrophe. Seeing that he was committed to what he called a bird in hand, they theorized that the more difficult it was for him to bring the girl over, the harder it would be for the two to get along, because it would be almost impossible for her to satisfy his expectations of a sufficiently submissive wife. Emmanuel did not appreciate their lack of support. He ignored them and hurried back home to retrieve his girl.

At the embassy, Emmanuel learned that the problem with Rose's papers seemed to be a major one and that he was dealing with it at the wrong locale, a US agency, where bribery was unknown. He and the girl returned to his hotel to regroup and re-strategize. He told her that he had a lot of running around to do and that he better do it in Lagos where everything was possible. All of this would involve money.

Emmanuel got Rose a different birth certificate. With that, she obtained a new passport based on the fingerprints and the personal information of someone from a minority tribe. Still, the US embassy, without explanation, refused to affix a visa to the new passport. Emmanuel went another route and tried to get her a student visa called an I-94. That effort also hit a roadblock.

WHEN ROSE'S PEOPLE found out that Emmanuel was ensconced in a hotel suite in Lagos with their daughter and had not bothered to visit their village to take care of the formalities that would have signaled the community that she was about to be a bride, they started a rumor campaign. They said he had no intention of marrying their daughter, and they would not talk of bringing her to America. They complained to everyone that Emmanuel was teaching their innocent child behavior inconsistent with the moral values she was raised to observe. They claimed he was just using her body for his pleasure, a grievous sin, if not a crime. He went to the village, bought goats for the chiefs and swore to anyone who would listen that he was an honorable man. "Prove it," they said, jeering at him. To show that they were wrong about him and his intentions, Emmanuel relocated to Nigeria the white wedding he had planned to celebrate in America. He placed paid announcements in newspapers and on radio about a US-based businessman joining a local college girl in holy matrimony.

The wedding was a grand event. Emmanuel's intent was to raise a lot of money from family, friends, and other invitees. With a huge stack of cash in his bank account, he theorized the US embassy would quickly issue his woman a special visa called an H1B, which allowed hundreds of businessmen from China and India to enter the United States to invest in and grow the American economy. But this strategy did not work either. After this third strike, he contracted with smugglers to bring Rose to America as a well-traveled businesswoman fleeing persecution from her country's military regime. The smugglers got her an international passport as a citizen of the oil-producing nation of Equatorial Guinea. Then, instead of flying her straight to the United States, they took her to Tanzania, Botswana, Burundi, and South Africa. From there she flew to Brazil, to Peru, and finally to Cuba.

As Emmanuel would recall later, Rose lived in some of those countries for months while the smugglers monitored the movements of US Border Patrol agents. Her hotel bills alone almost caused him to have cardiac arrest. But thank God for graduate school. He returned to school and signed up for yet another postgraduate degree. He had planned to use grants and loans to build himself a mansion in Africa. Now he used the money to finance his woman's coming to America. His African buddies, hearing that Emmanuel was spending money like a drunken sailor to bring an African woman to the United States, thought he was crazy to try a gamble on which other African men had lost their shirts. They too found out that their friend was not good at taking advice. He was good only at dispensing advice and words of wisdom to others. He ignored all the friends warning him about his African bride. He told them he was set on proving his detractors wrong when his girl reached Texas.

The day she finally arrived was a festive one. Emmanuel's African and American friends showed up at the airport, carrying balloons and placards with festoons. They draped the railings as if to welcome a head of state. They filled the arrival hall to welcome the much-anticipated queen to Texas. After that, the party moved to Emmanuel's town house. The men, who knew what their friend had endured in terms of spending and stress for two years, had gotten together and had killed a cow and several goats to prepare all kinds of African delicacies. At the all-day, all-night party, German beer flowed freely, loosening people's tongues. The DJ was so happy and excited for Emmanuel that he encouraged guests to toss dollars at him as he danced to defray the costs of the layaway.

The music was so loud that at the behest of neighbors who had to work the next day, the neighborhood-watch patrol team stopped by to ask that the music be turned down or that the party should be ended. Since a lot of adult beverages were still available, no one wanted to leave. It was two in the morning, and the party was just getting started. Someone approached the disc jockey and persuaded him to lower the volume.

With the music turned way down, partygoers could hear each other. That was when other African men with damaged egos and conspicuous scars from wife importation scams started swapping war stories. They admitted that no one held a gun to their heads to ditch their American wives for the African variety. And although they had not spent half as much money and time as Emmanuel had to import his woman, his situation was nothing short of déjà vu for them. They kept looking at the girl and at him out of the corners of their eyes, making mental comparisons. They focused on Emmanuel and the enormous belly that his African outfit could not completely hide, a protruding gut common to all African cab drivers at America's fourth-largest airport, who ate all night to keep awake while waiting for fares at Bush International.

On the other hand, though she was doing justice to assorted flavors of ice cream, Rose looked like she had stepped out of a French fashion catalog. Emmanuel's friends concluded that she was indeed a looker but not a keeper. The alcohol had sufficiently loosened up the men to liberate their tongues. They congratulated Emmanuel on his gallantry but told him his fight was just beginning. They reminded him that all of them were, through no fault of their own, divorced from the girls they had put on layaway at home and had spent plenty of dollars to import to the United States. They pleaded with him not to make the mistake of believing that since he had paid to bring the girl to America, she belonged exclusively to him. They provided him with a not-to-do list, which they said no one had bothered to give them when they were making fools of themselves.

First on the list: do not teach the girl to drive. The second and third items: do not let her obtain a driver's license or start college anytime soon. They advised Emmanuel to start making babies with his girl the moment the last guest left the tenement that morning; he should make sure she was a mother before turning her loose on the larger American society, they said.

Some of the men found that their investments in imported wives had not only failed to pay dividends but had turned them into enemies of their former in-laws back home, whom they felt had conned them. These men had come to the party prepared. Away from Rose, they handed Emmanuel a powdery substance that they claimed had the power to promote fertility in women through midlife, even those on the best birth-control pharmaceuticals devised by man. They advised him to spike her favorite foods and the water she drank and to sprinkle some on her bras, underwear, panty hose, cosmetics, lipstick, lotions, shampoos, bath soaps, and any other items her body would come in contact with. They assured Emmanuel that if he followed their prescription, being in the same room with the girl would be enough to immediately start forming babies inside of her. On the other hand they warned him that if he acted like a gentleman and did not heed their admonition to extract at least one child from her while she was still a greenhorn in America, as soon as she knew her way to the apartment complex's mailroom and back, she would skip town. They emphasized that since he would not be able to recoup his losses even if he sued her in court, his only recourse was to make a baby with her as a consolation return on his enormous investment.

His busybody advisers didn't know that Emmanuel had already purchased a red, two-door convertible so that his wife could go to school as soon as she got to the United States. Because he did not want to appear to be letting others run his house for him, he ignored their unsolicited counsel. He thought he saw a tinge of jealousy in the way his friends were looking at his wife. Emmanuel smiled at his good fortune and concluded that his friends, out of envy, were trying to sow doubts in his mind about a girl from an upstanding family who happened to be more beautiful than any woman any of those guys had ever called his own.

Emmanuel enrolled Rose in school full time. At the end of the first semester, he testified to those who had been calling him to check on the status of his marriage that a decent and properly raised African girl like his wife would never betray a man who had stood so firmly beside her and who had spent so much capital to bring her to the land of milk and honey, the United States of America.

Because Rose did not have to work, she attended school day and night. In less than two years she became a registered nurse. Friends of Emmanuel working in the health care industry and members of her support group, including other African women she had met in school, managed to hook her up with the ideal job. She worked Monday through Friday and was off on weekends. Rose wanted to work a second job to send money to her parents, who wrote often, asking her for help to pay for her younger siblings' education.

Meanwhile, Emmanuel, who had been ready to start making babies, changed his mind. He got Rose an organic-chemistry tutor, hoping she would go for a master's degree in nursing, which might come in handy since he was planning to open a home-health business. She surprised him by saying she saw no reason having children should conflict with school. Rose said she could handle both simultaneously. Therefore, with her consent, Emmanuel put the sports car up for sale and bought her a four-door import. She drove the cars to work interchangeably. After a while, Rose told him that her driving was too unsteady for her to safely operate the bigger of the two vehicles. She said it was much easier for her to maneuver the smaller car and to park it at her assigned space at work. She asked Emmanuel to hold off on selling it until they needed a car with room for a baby seat or two.

Rose didn't tell him that driving a different car every day made her look like a nurse who had made it big and was working in the health care industry only because she was a compassionate human being. That perception made her the envy of coworkers, particularly those without reliable transportation and others riding buses to work. Whenever they had the chance, they told her how blessed she was. To confirm this sentiment, she let that blessing trickle down on them. Every day after work, she gave a lift to at least one of the bus riders. Sometimes she gave them a ride to work from their apartments or their bus stops. That was how she and her coworkers became fast friends. They talked freely, sharing their best-kept secrets.

Some of Rose's friends were the curious types and asked about her personal life. How many kids did she have? None, she told them. Why? They asked. Was she waiting for an act of Congress before fulfilling the commandment to go forth and multiply? She said there was method to her madness. She told them that before she left Africa, an oracle had prophesied that the man who brought her overseas was not her rightful husband but merely a conduit to facilitate her coming to America. She said it was also prophesied that her rightful and permanent husband was waiting for her somewhere in the States. For that reason, she told her friends, since she had been in the United States she had terminated what she called three wrong pregnancies.

"And how did your husband take the news that he was merely a filler husband?" one friend asked.

Rose replied that she had this temporary husband wrapped around her little finger, to the extent that he took whatever she bothered to tell him as gospel.

"Not only has he never worked in the health care industry, but he has this huge chip on his shoulder and thinks that nursing is an unglamorous job meant for women only. Therefore most things medical sail over his head. So it is piece of cake to con him about anything having to do with anatomy and physiology. I just cook up some mumbo-jumbo medical jargon, and voilà, he's convinced that my pregnancy terminations were spontaneous miscarriages. I told him that they were caused by ovarian failures that resulted because the excessive heat from his body practically fried his seed. I said this indicated our endocrinological incompatibility. I also convinced him that my doctor said that the less we share the bedroom, the better the chance of the next pregnancy reaching full term."

Rose's friends, being Southern Baptists, were properly aghast and told her so. She hushed them up by discussing natural selection and how it improves species. They didn't understand her explanation, so she watered it down. She said she was not going to make the mistake of creating babies with a stranger who was not the permanent husband she was destined to find in America.

Rose's friends lied and said they were not concerned about her husband but about her and her health. They said they worried that given the reality that women were not provided with an unlimited number of eggs, her choice of birth control was too risky, inefficient, and expensive, not to mention immoral. Rose replied that it baffled her that she kept getting pregnant despite being on the best birth-control pill on the market. She also revealed the things she was doing physically and spiritually to force her facilitator to fall deeply in love with another woman and to leave her alone so she could concentrate on finding her true soul mate.

CHAPTER 2

MAYBE IT WAS the usual suspect, jealousy, or maybe it was a sense that they had a duty to right the world's wrongs, but some of Rose's American-born coworkers sought to lessen her husband's financial pain and the indignity of running from endocrinologists to radiologists to urologists, getting poked, diced, and sliced in a search for problems that didn't exist. They sought out Emmanuel and told him that the miscarriages his wife had reported were a cynical ploy. He did not believe them and was suspicious of their intentions. They sensed that he was deeply in love with Rose and begged him not to expose them and damage their friendship with her.

Months later, Emmanuel returned from work one day and found that there was no light in the house. He turned on all the light switches and the breakers he could feel in the dark. Nothing! He concluded that there was a power outage. He called Rose at work to find out what had happened. Coworkers informed him that according to the schedule Rose had been at home for the past two days because of a stomach virus.

Emmanuel rushed to the utility company office to pay the bill, but he was told no bill was due. So why was power cut off at his place? The company apologized for its mistake and gave him a discount voucher to apply toward the next month's bill. He went back home and watched television. Soon after, Rose returned and started dinner. While the food was cooking, she soaked in the bathtub. She did not eat much. Emmanuel asked if she was feeling all right. Rose said her supervisors had overworked her in preparation for a certification visit by state inspectors. She told him she needed to go straight to bed to regain her strength.

Rose woke up early the next morning to iron Emmanuel's shirt. She cheerfully fixed his favorite breakfast: blueberry muffins, pancakes, over-easy eggs, and bacon. She took out the trash, brought in the newspaper and placed it on the dining room table, and stepped into the bathroom to check her makeup. Then she put on her scrubs and headed out to the carport. Emmanuel, who was playing possum while his wife was getting ready to leave the house, got up and went to the window to observe her as she drove off.

An hour and a half later, he conducted an experiment. He called her job. The front desk transferred him to the nurses' station. Emmanuel was told she was not there. He insisted she was and asked to speak to a supervisor. He was transferred to the supervisor for that shift. The nurse consulted the weekly schedule and told Emmanuel that Rose had asked to take the day off to nurse a virus but would return to work the next day. Emmanuel suggested that perhaps the boss lady was misreading the schedule. She asked if he was a physician. He replied that he was not. She asked if he was a patient. He said he was not. With those bases covered, she took offense and loudly berated him for trying to tell her how to do her job, considering that he was neither a clinical person nor a paying customer. After daring him to sue her and the hospital, she hung up on him.

Emmanuel was confused about what was going on. According to her supervisor, Rose was off, but for the last three days, she had left the house bright and early to go to work. What job had she been going to? The answer was not clear. He had always been an admirer of science, so he refused to jump to conclusions when all the facts were not available. He did not want to raise any alarm, false or otherwise, particularly since he needed to show the world that he was still in that phase when love was supposed to cover all iniquities, no matter how many and how serious. He told himself that his wife was the most beautiful woman this side of heaven, and so all men who set eyes on her were jealous of his good fortune.

Emmanuel rose to his feet and spoke loudly to convince himself that all was well. He sat down briefly, but his mind would not rest. He told himself that this situation was a tempest in a teacup and would pass. He rationalized that Rose might have landed a second job and forgotten to tell him about it. He got dressed and set off for work. He was glad to leave the house, which depressed him, but he could not turn off his mind. He tried to work, but even casual acquaintances noticed that he looked spaced out and asked if he was all right. Though Emmanuel mumbled that he was okay, he wondered about the sincerity of his answer because deep down inside, he felt growing doubt. He left just before lunch to visit his wife's workplace.

Emmanuel arrived about the time first-shift workers were taking their lunch break. He looked around for familiar faces but saw none. The two nurses who had tried to be his friends were not there.

An impatient security officer, mistaking Emmanuel for one of the new hires due for job orientation that morning, shoved him into the break room before he had the chance to introduce himself. Across from where he sat, some nurses, not realizing how loudly they gossiped, were talking about how fortunate Rose was.

After the nurses returned to work, another batch entered the break room. Emmanuel visited with two standing by the vending machine, trying to decide whether to buy snacks or super-size energy drinks. He inquired about Rose. They told him the same thing he was told on the phone: she was off duty but would be back at work the next day, a Thursday. He was a bit ticked off because although they would not admit it, he thought the women knew who he was and had conspired to play a practical joke on him. If they were playing games, he did not appreciate being made a target.

Emmanuel abruptly turned to leave. Forgetting to have his parking ticket validated, he returned to the garage and got in his car. When he reached the exit, he realized he had made a mistake that would cost him a couple of dollars. Because his ticket wasn't validated, the gate would not rise to let him out. He popped opened the ashtray and the glove compartment. As he was fishing for coins to put in the machine, a young lady in scrubs approached and signaled for him to roll down his window. Emmanuel was too preoccupied with his thoughts to notice, but when she knocked on the passenger-side window, he lowered it.

"Yes?" he said impatiently.

"Mister, if I give you a little gas money will you give me a ride a couple of blocks down the street?"

Emmanuel looked at his watch to make sure he had enough time to be A Good Samaritan and still make it back to his job on time.

"Pretty please, sir? I know it's a bother, but it's raining cats and dogs and I need to get to my other job on the other side of town.

He looked up and noticed that it was indeed pouring outside of the parking garage.

"Sure!" he replied.

"Thank you, sir."

"Don't mention it. Where are you going?"

"I am going to the bus stop."

"And where is your bus stop, ma'am?"

"Make a right at that light in front of us. At Ben Taube Street, hang a left. Next, make a right at the second light and a right at the one after that. The bus stop is on Holcombe Boulevard. You can't miss it, but if you get to the Kettle Restaurant, you've gone too far."

Emmanuel was not listening to her instructions. He was rummaging in the glove compartment and paying more attention to the drivers behind him. He finally found enough money to feed the meter, and the arm on the machine shot up to let his car pass. He sped out of the garage and turned left on a red light, prompting the drivers who had the right of way to swerve and to blast their horns at him.

"Sir, please turn on your windshield wiper and your defroster. Our breath is fogging up your windows. I suspect that is the reason you couldn't see that the light you just went through was red. You did not seem to notice the other drivers either, and they had the right of way."

"May I remind you that this is a free ride? I don't need the driver-training if you do not mind my saying so."

"It's raining, for goodness' sake. You need to slow down. Most of the motorists in this city do not know how to adjust their driving to accommodate inclement weather. I am sorry to say that you are one of them, and you are putting both of our lives in jeopardy."

"How old are you?"

"I do not see how that matters."

"I am a good driver. I have been driving longer than you have been alive, okay?"

"Right, as if the graveyards in this city are not full of drivers who used to exude such pristine confidence in their driving abilities. Thank God this is not Main Street where even making a right turn when you have the green light is deadly. That illegal left turn you made would have cost you a lot, and I am not talking about just money. Please start driving like an adult. Do not insist on having your way while you are driving. You are not a child, okay? The road does not belong to you alone. If your defogger does not work, let's roll down the windows. I am not a lump of salt. I do not mind getting wet from the rain as long as we make it to my bus stop alive. Did I mention that I have to get home to meet my kids as they get off the school bus, to feed them, and to help them with their homework? I won't get the chance to do all those chores if I end up in a mortuary this afternoon."

Emmanuel turned on all the lights, including the ones inside the car, and set the wipers on the fastest speed.

"Sir, please defog the windshield so we can see where we are going."

As Emmanuel fumbled with the dials on the dashboard, he got distracted. Instead of turning right on Fannie Boulevard, he continued straight ahead across railroad tracks onto Main Street.

"Sir, are you all right?" his passenger asked nervously.

"Yes, I am. What makes you think I am not all right?"

"Well, for starters, you just missed hitting a metro train."

"A train? Where?"

"Yes, a train. Back there."

"Are you sure?"

"Of course I am sure. The average metro train is about two blocks long. I do not see how you didn't notice that one."

"Those people drive those things entirely too slowly if you ask me."

"Maybe so, but it is a federal law. Even in rural East Texas, except at an authorized railroad crossing, you are not at liberty to cross a railroad track. And you, sir, have just crossed three. What is your emergency?"

"Who said anything about an emergency?"

"Actions speak louder than words. Sir, am I making you nervous?"

"No, you are not. Why do you ask?"

"Because you just cut in front of a school bus."

"I am all right."

"No, sir, you are not all right. You are driving with cabin lights on. You are not paying attention to other road users or to your surroundings. Your hands are sweating. You are talking to yourself. And your eyes are glazed. When we get to the Kettle Restaurant, please pull into the parking lot and let me check your blood pressure. Something is going on with you, and you need to find out what it is before you hurt yourself or others."

"Thank for offering unsolicited medical advice to a very healthy man, one who jogs at least three miles every morning, but I must get back to my job now. I regret having to cancel this emergency appointment with you."

"Sir, you do not understand."

"What is that I do not understand?"

"You do not seem to understand the mechanics of your body."

"That is true. Microbiology was not in my school curriculum."

"I am sorry to hear that, but is something depressing you?"

"Like what?"

"Well, it could be anything."

"Depression is an American thing. Where I come from we do not know what depression is."

"Regardless, something is upsetting you. You look as frazzled as someone who has been tortured with sleep deprivation. You need to disconnect yourself from whatever is depressing you. You need to decompress."

"All right, ma'am. That is what I am going to do. See you later."

"Okay, if you do not want me to check your blood pressure, which I bet is high, why not sit in your car and rest until what I suspect is an anxiety episode passes? If you stay on the road now, you will be a danger to yourself and others."

"Thanks, but unlike you I am not on salary. I get paid by the hour, so I have to get back to work now if that is okay with you."

"Are you sure you are in a condition to operate this car safely?"

"Is that your final question?"

"Yes, it is."

"Then my answer is yes, I am sure I can operate this car so long as the *D* on the dashboard's gear selector stands for 'drive' and the *P* stands for 'park.' Thanks for asking."

"Thanks for the ride. I will check on you tomorrow when I come to work. By the way, my name is Mary. What section do you work in and on which floor?"

"I am sorry. Your assumption is incorrect. I do not work at the hospital. I came there to check on somebody, but she was not there."

"Who were you looking for?"

"Rose Awak-Isang."

"Oh, you must be the older brother who she said sponsored her coming to America. You must be very happy for her now that your brother-in-law, who has been calling her at the job every day, has finally come from California to spend some quality time with her."

"She forgot to mention that to me. How long did she say he would be town?"

"Three days. But do not quote me on that. I am not one of those overpaid registered nurses. I just do all the work. After I have worked my fingers to the bone, they saunter in, take the credit, and get the big bucks. But I overheard them saying that your sister should be returning to work from her mini-emergency honeymoon Thursday, which is tomorrow."

"They said that?"

"What a minute. Why do I feel like I am your primary source of information about this? African siblings, unlike we Americans, are supposed to be very close to each other. You live in the same house with your little sister, and you know nothing about her love life? What gives? That is not how a family is supposed to function, not even in America. Anyway, please remember to drive safely for yourself and for others."

"Thanks, mom. I will keep that in mind."

"Sir, you did not have to be sarcastic with me. It may not look like it, but I want nothing from you. I am a nurse aide in the order of Florence Nightingale. For those of us following in the footsteps of that extraordinary Englishwoman, nursing is not a career or a profession but a calling. We care for people. We are healers. We reduce hurt. I know that it looks like I'm bossing you, but I do not want you to do damage to life and property and be haunted for the rest of your life. I work. That means I can take care of myself. I am not trying to get you to pay my rent, okay?"

"I am sorry if I have hurt your feelings, Mary. I was not thinking. I know you meant well. Forgive me."

"That's okay. You are forgiven. Just do not get into traffic until you are sufficiently calmed. Try not to hurt others because you are hurt."

"I promise."

A bus pulled up at the stop, and Mary boarded it to go to her second job. Then it dawned on her that because it was a weekday she had to go home to get her kids ready for school before she could head to the nursing home. She hurriedly pulled the cable and asked the bus driver to let her out at the next stop, a block away.

Emmanuel returned to his job but could not concentrate enough to work. He looked so ashen leaving the men's room that his supervisor stopped by to ask if he was all right. Emmanuel said he had eaten something at lunch that did not agree with him. The boss suggested that the potato salad, which had been sitting outside of the freezer for a while, was the most likely culprit. He was sympathetic and said a little rest might do Emmanuel a lot of good. Since it was raining, the boss gave Emmanuel a ride to the parking lot and permission to take the rest of the day off.

It was still raining when Emmanuel got home. He went straight to bed since he could not decide how he would react to his wife when she walked through the front door. But he was certain of one thing. He would not ask anyone for advice about the evolving situation. Emmanuel had found that in talking to people when his mind was on overload, he would divulge information that made him look foolish. At this point, silence was golden. He did not want to talk to his buddies, particularly the ones who were still happily married to their American wives. They had told him there was no need to go through the hassle of traveling to Africa to put a woman on layaway, returning to America to work two-and-a-half jobs, and sending the woman money to spend on the boyfriends she had before her sponsor showed up with bags of dollars. If he let such people know about the state of his home, they would remind him that just as a bad woman is never changed by her location, a good woman is a good woman no matter where she was born and raised. He had confidently rejected these admonitions.

Rose returned at 5.25 p.m., the time she usually arrived when she did not have to shop for food. She brought in bags of grocery, however, put them on the kitchen counter, and dashed in to use the bathroom in the hallway. After washing her hands, she put away the groceries.

She had expected Emmanuel to be in the living room, as was his habit, watching the tail end of the local news before the *NBC Nightly News* with Tom Brokaw. But Emmanuel was not there. She went into the bedroom and discovered him in bed under the comforter. Rose greeted him, but he did not answer. She stepped out of her uniform, balled it up, and threw it into the hamper. Then she peeled off the comforter and spoke to him again.

"It's almost five-thirty. You are not watching the news, and you are in bed early. Are you all right?"

"How was your day?"

"I'm glad that they do this stupid inspection at the hospital only once a year. This one got us running like crazy. I'm glad it's over. To celebrate, I went to the fish market in Kemah. I got you your favorites, wild salmon and freshwater trout. Do you want me to make you stew or pepper soup with the salmon or with the other fish?"

"Neither. I am not hungry."

"What's wrong?"

"A little sour stomach. But otherwise, in the immortal words of soul brother number one James Brown, I feel good."

"Then you should not be in bed this early. Who fed you what?"

"Something I ate at lunch did not agree with me. My boss thought it was a virus and panicked. He did not want to risk decimating his workforce, so he sent me home early. I am well-rested now."

"That virus has met its match. I've got something to stop it in its tracks. But first let me run to the store to stock up on soups. This is a war that must be waged on all fronts."

"Don't bother. Our side has won already. The clinic at work gave me some pinkish potion and told me not to take anything else for at least twenty-four hours. Besides, you just came in from work. You deserve a break, not more work babying your husband. Please do not worry about me. Sit down and rest your feet. Are you off tomorrow?"

"No, I'm not. I wish I was."

"So relax. Go take a bath. Soak in the tub. Get some rest."

"Okay. Thanks."

Rose got into the shower and shampooed and highlighted her hair. After a while, she peeked out of the shower to confirm that Emmanuel was asleep. His loud snoring signaled that he was. When she was done in the bathroom, instead of turning on the hair dryer as she usually did, she tiptoed out, shut the bedroom door behind her, and took her hair dryer to the living room. That was a good excuse not to lay down beside her husband. In the living room, she dried her hair in peace while taking in a little TV.

The next day Rose reported to her job glowing. She was so radiant that her friends could not wait for the break time to come so she could tell them everything that had happened. She did not disappoint them when the break finally arrived.

CHAPTER 3

EMMANUEL HAD TIME over the weekend to wrap his mind around all that had happened during the week. He seemed to have made peace with himself. He was so calmed that he did not fume when he took out the trash and noticed that his car was gone from the carport. Rose's car was there. Emmanuel saw why, but it did not upset him: the sticker and the front license plate on her car were missing. What else could go wrong? He went back into the house and got a paper towel. He popped the hood and pulled out the dipstick. There was barely enough oil to cover a house fly's foot. He got a jacket and his wallet and headed to an auto-parts store for a few quarts of SAE 5W-30 motor oil.

Just as Emmanuel pulled into traffic, a car he had not seen magically appeared behind him, flashing blue-and-red lights. He moved over to let the police car pass, but the cruiser did no such thing. An authoritative voice from the PA instructed him to turn into the driveway ahead. He complied. An officer approached Emmanuel's car and asked to see his driver's license and evidence of insurance coverage. He produced the documents. The officer asked why he was operating an automobile in Texas without authorization. Emmanuel explained that the vehicle was usually driven by his wife but was registered in his name. He told the officer that someone may have liberated the car of its sticker while it was parked at her job. The officer returned to his squad car. After some time, he came back and issued Emmanuel a warning.

After Emmanuel had replenished the oil, he drove to a county courthouse to get replacement sticker before another police officer pulled him over.

While driving on Main Street, Emmanuel passed several flower shops with Valentine's Day displays, and Mary came to mind. He decided that she was indeed a caring person, a good resource to have. He felt bad that life had been unfair to her. Though she worked hard, he could tell from her voice that she was struggling. She was underwater with no relief in sight. He felt terrible about the way he had allowed his problem to dictate the way he had treated her. He had no right to have contributed to her burden. Since he was in the part of town where she worked, Emmanuel decided to send her a bouquet of roses to make up for treating her so shabbily. As luck would have it, when he turned a corner, he saw Mary sitting at a bus-stop bench, reading a newspaper. He honked his horn. She looked up briefly and returned to her paper. He hollered. She looked up from the paper again. He beckoned her, but she did not move. He drove away, parked the car, and walked back to the bus stop.

"Hello, Mary. That was me trying to get your attention."

"Oh hi, Emmanuel."

"Are you deaf in one ear?"

"No. I have perfect hearing in both ears. Was that you hollering at me? I did not recognize the voice. What's up?"

"It is a workday. What are you doing at the bus stop now?"

"I'm waiting for the fifty-six bus, and it is taking forever to get here."

"Why are you waiting for a bus when you should be at work making money? Did you switch shifts or move up in the ranks and get the big bucks?"

"Not to my knowledge! But I do believe in miracles."

"Then why are you waiting for a bus during work hours?"

"My thirteen-year-old got into an argument with her teacher. Instead of whipping her butt and making her sit down and learn like schools used to do in the old days, they summoned me to an emergency conference with her teacher. So I am taking an early lunch break to go to the school."

"If you want, I can run you to the school and back in time for you to grab lunch."

"Thanks, but no."

"What do you mean by that? I thought we parted as friends last time."

"Have you changed? Has your driving undergone a major transformation?"

"What do you mean?"

"I am so sorry for my lack of clarity. But in plain English, are you still driving like a daredevil?"

"Please do not start that again."

"Is that a yes or a no?"

"It is neither."

"No, seriously, do you mean to say that the state of Texas is so wrapped up in ensuring no hard-drugs enters any part of the United States from Mexico that it has forgotten to watch the videos of your driving and to suspend your license for the rest of your natural life?"

"Stop your stand-up comedy. We are wasting valuable time. You know that middle schools are not twenty-four-hour-a-day enterprises. Let's go before this one adjourns for the day."

"I know this might sound self-serving, but I like to arrive at my destination in one piece. Given the way you drive, I may arrive at a morgue instead of at my child's school. So if the bus is not coming today, I would prefer to walk to the school than to ride in a car with you as a driver. But thanks for offering."

"Buses take too long. You should know that by now. I could save you time."

"Yes, I understand, but according to King Solomon, time means nothing to the dead."

"I am a licensed driver."

"Hush. Do not let any state personnel hear you make that claim. They would think they have been derelict in the performance of their statutory duty to this great state. What you have is not state-issued. At least it should not be, given the way you drive. Grocery store licenses do not count in Texas. They are not testimonials to good driving. They are for check-cashing purposes only."

"It is safe to say that you have a morbid fear of death."

"No, I am not afraid of dying. In case you have not noticed, I am a nurse by profession. I work in nursing homes. I have been around the dead and the dying a good while. No, I'm not scared of death. What I am afraid of is untimely death, dying without some type of warning. Wrecks have been notorious for that kind of death. That is the way my husband—well, the father of my children—died, and it messed up a whole lot of things for me. So my preference is to die on a weekend at home of some sickness. My paternal grandma used to refer to that as a gradual transition: a little sickness followed by a build-up, then death."

"What?"

"If any family member or A Good Samaritan wants to help the orphans, it would be easier if all my kids were in one location, preferably at home. On the other hand, if the authorities have to scrape my remains from the street on a weekday, my kids will come back from school, and no one will be there to let them into the house. That would be very disruptive to the structure they are used to. They would roam about like sheep without a shepherd. The only one who would be blissful about that is my thirteen-year-old, the one I'm on my way to strangle."

"Well, death is disruptive all right, but your obsessive fear of it won't let you see all that life is offering you. You are young. Moreover, you are alive today. Take advantage of your situation. Enjoy the free gift of life. Even if you are up to your neck in debt and are beset with knee and joint problems like I am, it does not matter. So long as you are breathing, those problems are minor and conquerable. You have plenty of time to set your affairs in order whether you have money or not. But first things first: enjoy today. Second, be positive. I guarantee you the future will be better for you than your past has been. Life is set up like that."

"I'm well aware that I have nothing remotely resembling an estate that my kids could inherit when I am gone, but I would like to have time to straighten up my house and put everything in order before I die. I also would use that time to finally make entries in my journal. I have been so busy trying to put food on the table and to keep my daughter out of trouble that I have not been able to write in my journal each day. I hate to leave a mess behind. I was raised by a very organized set of parents."

"You keep a journal?"

"Yes. Is that a surprise?"

"That's very impressive. These days most young Americans would not be caught dead with pens in their possession, and you keep a journal?"

"Yes, but it is not a physical journal yet. Right now all the entries are in hieroglyphics in my head. But I intend to transcribe everything into the journal during the sabbatical before my last breath. I cannot afford to catch a ride with you and risk dying in a wreck before I complete that important project."

"Okay, let's go. My car is just around the corner."

"Where is the notarized guarantee that I am going to arrive in one piece?"

"I have full insurance coverage on this car."

"What does that mean to a single mom with school-age kids?"

"That means that in case of a wreck, whether I am at fault or the other driver is, you would be covered bumper to bumper."

"Hey, are you saying that I am fat?"

"Let's go, please. I promise to protect you."

"You are so chivalrous, so old-fashioned! I like that in my knight."

Emmanuel and Mary walked from the bus stop to his car. He went around to the left side and opened the door for her. She got in, sat down, snapped on the seat belt, and then unclicked the seat belt and got out of the car as quickly as she had entered. She looked like she had been stung by a scorpion.

"What's wrong now?" Emmanuel asked.

"Do you know that you are driving a car without a state license in an area of the city that has more police officers than civilians, an area many people would not choose to visit on their own?"

"So?"

"So? This may come as surprise to you, but I do not want to go to prison. So let me wait for the bus while you go straight to the courthouse and take care of your business with the state of Texas, okay?"

"You are so dramatic. Has anyone ever told you that you worry too much?"

"Being cautious and insisting on being safe do not constitute worrying."

"You, my friend, are a certified worrier."

"Not according to my father. He used to say that if you live in the great state of Texas, you will undoubtedly learn that erring on the side of caution is a sound investment of time, energy, and money. It is not at all the same thing as worrying."

"But you do worry too much."

"Like lots of Africans, some of my neighbors say that they are too focused on the outcome to be concerned with the process. It must be a cultural thing that y'all do not know how to be orderly and to wait your turns. You just walk up to the head of a line without noticing that other people have been waiting. You people take too many risks. When you drive, you constantly cut in front of people who could fire their weapons at you if you catch them on a bad day.

"I am an American. Therefore, the American thing to do, particularly if you are a parent, is to consider the consequences of your actions before, not after, you've taken them. Otherwise, it won't be long before someone from child protective services shows up and convinces a family-court judge that your kids would be better off if they were taken from you, separated, and sent to different foster homes. Listen to me. Risk evaluation is an industry in America."

"You make parenting sound like an impossible mission, so hard, so lacking in joy."

"Obviously you do not have kids yet, but I do. If I die and my kids are all in one location, someone who is fighting the good fight, as the Apostle Paul puts it, will have sympathy and take them in. If am taken to prison, everyone will curse me and rather than help my kids, will tell them that I am an example of a bad mother. I know that I am not educated enough in symbolic logic to adequately derive my conclusion from the premise, but how does ending up in jail make me an example of a good parent?"

"The short answer is that no one is going to jail, at least not on my account. The long answer is that help is available for your kids' pickups and drop-offs. I know the principal of a day care place called Day Bridge Center. I also know the owners of a child care facility called Precious Graceful Land Academy. These places not only accept a government voucher called NCI, but they will provide buses to transport your kids safely home. See? Help is available. Therefore you do not have to be running from pillar to post as you have been doing. I'm surprised that you have not had a heart attack. Slow down and get the help. They do not yet have awards for single mothers who burn through their energy reserves and die of natural causes before their kids are out of middle school."

"Please do not change the subject."

"I am not changing the subject. I just want you to know that life is good for those who look for it to be good. And as Saint Francis of Assisi said, God's helpers are everywhere for us when we hit turbulence or struggle in the valley of the shadow of death. So if you get in touch with one of these places I just told you about, they will help with transportation for your children, and your schedule will not have to be as hard on you as it has been."

"I am certain now that you do not have kids. There is no way you will understand the trials and the temptations of parenting until you become a parent. If I go the attractive, easy-on-the-body day care route, my kids would get home before I do. That would be bad news for what my father used to call moral rectitude. There would be days, plenty of them, when my thirteen-year-old would not make it home."

"What do you mean?"

"Right now, she waits and rides the same bus with her siblings. That gives me time to be home before they are. Though she is the oldest, I've asked the younger ones to keep their eyes on her for me when my children are away from home and my supervision. They are doing a fantastic job. They force her to be on her best behavior so she won't get snitched on. When my children get home, I am there with supper. Before I leave for my second job, I instruct them that no one is to leave the house except if asked to do so by a firefighter. I tell them no one is permitted to make a store run, because I've left them all kinds of snacks in the cabinets. All they have to do is finish their home work, eat, brush their teeth, take a bath, read scripture, and then hit the sack. That way the thirteen-year-old, who looks a lot like a woman, as I did when I was that age, does not get the chance to do the crazy things I did and end up not finishing high school. But let's get back to the subject of driving. In Texas, operating a motor vehicle without a proper license is a prison offense."

"I said that no one is going to jail, not on account of me."

"You still do not understand."

"Please read this." Emmanuel handed Mary a piece of paper.

"What is it?"

"Please just read it, okay?"

"If this piece of paper is not the deed to a huge house in a gated community, how is it going to keep the good people at child protective services from taking away my kids the moment I have been shackled, placed in the backseat of a police cruiser, and transported to the big house for my bad judgment in joy riding in an automobile not properly registered and licensed and therefore probably stolen?"

As they were driving away, Emmanuel replied, "That paper was given to me by a state trooper, a member of the most elite law enforcement outfit in this state. He pulled me over this morning. After he looked into the state data bank and found that the vehicle was properly registered, he agreed that someone had pilfered the sticker from my windshield. He did not issue me a citation, just a warning to get a replacement sticker before the week is out. That is the beauty of American laws. Those enforcing them try not to break them while ensuring compliance."

Within a few minutes, they arrived at the courthouse, and Emmanuel found a parking spot across the street.

"Wait for me here. I will be right back," Emmanuel said. He jumped out of the automobile and ran to the other side of the street.

"What do you think you're doing, mister?" Mary hollered.

"I am going to the courthouse. What do you think I am doing?" Emmanuel hollered back.

"You can't park here. Come back here this instant," Mary said. She opened her door and appeared set to run across the street. Emmanuel raced back to the car.

"What is your problem, madam?"

"Who do you think you are, the governor of Texas?"

"No, you tell me who you think you are. Are you the state's chief parking attendant?"

"No, sir. I am not even the meter lady, but whatever my status, I'm unwilling to take a foolish risk."

"And I am not asking you to take one."

"Yes, you are."

"No, I'm not."

"Then look up. Do you see that bright-red neon sign flashing above your head?"

"Yes."

"Now read it."

"Why? Is this a literacy test that people with foreign accents must pass before they are can be fully integrated into American society?"

"Very funny! I know the sign is in American English, neither your language of birth or of choice, but that sign clearly says 'No Parking.' In America, *no* is a complete sentence. It requires no explanation. The only person who can park here without consequence to his pocketbook is the chief executive officer of this state, and he can do it only if accompanied by police officers dressed in knee-high boots and riding on powerful, ground-shaking motorcycles with flashing lights. Other mortals, that would be you and I, without exception, will be towed away and will get a ticket for violating the sanctity of this pricey real estate."

"That is the reason I told you to stay in the car while I ran into the courthouse, quickly handled my business, and returned. Why do you equate that simple request with being asked to do something immoral, illegal, and fattening?

"It maybe because it is all those things and more."

"It is not even close."

"You've got me jacked up."

"What do you mean by that?"

"You do not think I have any common sense left after having so many babies at a young age and out of wedlock, do you?"

"Ma'am, I do not know where you are heading with that train of thought. This spot is a dedicated loading zone for delivery drivers. They do not get cited for parking here to drop off legal papers in the courthouse. All I am asking you to do is remain in the car to give the impression the car is not parked. In this city, they do not tow a car when a live human is sitting in it. Pretend that I'm making a delivery, and we will not be towed."

"But you are not making a delivery."

"Yes I am. I am making a delivery and a pickup. I am delivering this money and a renewal notice to the county clerk and picking up a state document."

"Either you do not know how this downtown works, or you like to give away your money. Downtowns in this state are designed to make some people rich at the expense of others. The plan is to hurt your pocketbook."

"Me, give my money away to the government?"

"Yes, and it is all legal. By city ordinance, a tow from a public space is supposed to be authorized by the police. If everybody went by the book, a tow truck driver would not lower his equipment onto your bumper whenever and wherever he feels like it. But with the advent of high-tech towing equipment, he does not need to get out of his truck to do a tow. He could be parked a block away, but with a combo of a boom and a claw-like device, he could scoop up your car if he feels you parked illegally. On his way to a storage yard located on the other side of the big airport, he might notify a friendly traffic cop, who would approve the tow in absentia."

"Please get back into the car. There is no line in the county clerk's office at this hour to delay me and give an opportunistic tow truck driver time to descend on my car."

"There is more than enough time for the vultures to take your vehicle right under your nose. As I said, the towing business has evolved. It has not only gone corporate, attracting investors who expect hefty profits, but it has also gone high tech. Even as we speak, tow operators are scanning this area with surveillance gadgets. You park, they tow. I bet you my lunch money that the moment you step away from the car and cross the street again to the courthouse, half a dozen tow trucks will be lowering their booms on your car. In the old days, you would be tipped off on seeing them with yellow lights flashing, jumping curbs, driving on the shoulders, and racing down here. Now, with no warning and in the twinkling of an eye, your car will be on the way to a storage lot with me inside. By the way, do you have the title to this car and does it have your name on it?"

"You are so pessimistic. Do you think this is a stolen car?"

"I do not know that for a fact, so I would not speculate and draw that conclusion. But generally, because tow operators live on Mount Olympus and are above the traffic and property laws of this land, when your car gets towed, in addition to shaking you down for at least three hundred bucks, your torturers will demand to see your blood type, your DNA genome, and your original Social Security card. You will have to produce the car's blue title too. That state-issued document has to bear your name, or you will not get your car back. Do you understand?"

"You are an unreconstructed, natural worrier."

"No, I'm not. This is the Deep South. As is typical of Southerners, I choose to err on the side of caution. We are conservatives. That's all."

"Where did you say you're from again?"

"I am from the area of the state that is poised to make this nation the number-one producer of crude oil in the world. Why?"

"In other words, you are from a small town. I see the reason you are so paranoid at the sight of a police cruiser. Small-town Texas has left you seriously spooked. Please relax. You are now in the oil capital of the world. Its police department fights real crimes like embezzlement, malfeasance in high places, double dipping by foreign-born doctors, and Medicare and Medicaid fraud. It does not have the luxury of too much free time. Therefore, when you see officers on their beats doing what their former boss, Police Chief Lee P. Brown, called community policing, remain calm. That slogan by Scotland Yard in London, 'Police officers are your best friends,' is a reality in this town. Police in this city won't read you the riot act just because your windshield sticker is expired by a couple hours. They are very good at what they do. They even have a special unit to calm down jittery and panicky citizens like you.

"However, if you find yourself in small cities that do not have huge taxes bases, it is perfectly okay to start shaking in your boots if you make a wrong turn. If you are a Catholic, you might start reciting a combination of 'Ave Maria' and 'Nunc dimittis.' These cities seem to use their police departments as fundraising arms. Officers misuse their discretion. They do not need a reason to pull you over. And as I said, if one of them pulls you over, start panicking, for within five minutes, five other cruisers will surround you, giving the impression of a police state. Not so here in the energy capital of the world. Though police here also have the much-coveted discretion, they are careful about how they swing that nightstick. They do not want to end up making you rich by encouraging a suit for profiling. Therefore, they slap handcuffs on you and respectfully chauffeur you to jail only after they have checked with the city attorney to ensure that the arrest can withstand any legal challenge you and your attorney may bring."

"How long have you lived in my area of the state that you know so much about its sins and shortcomings?"

"Me?"

"Who else is here?"

"I never lived there. I am a city boy. I do not live in small towns."

"What then gives you the authority to state your opinions as facts?"

"Have you ever heard how canaries warn miners of the presence of potentially dangerous gas in mine shafts? Job fairs and friends have been the canaries for me when it comes to your costly town. I have been there for so many job fairs that I am virtually a resident. My friends who live there tell me all the time that everything costs too much and that all it takes to start living in your car is a cut in overtime hours. They also say that the town comes to standstill after just a little rain. The place has no drainage system. Agreed? A little rain brings floods and causes accidents."

"My town puts America on top of the world with its wealth of oil. The potential is there to make money whether you are an employee or an employer. You cannot say that about most small cities."

"Yes, but the place is so expensive that most workers cannot afford to move their families there. They are forced to keep two homes. They work around the clock just to keep up. My friends tell me that if and when they drive to work in neighboring New Mexico, they are followed by small-town police and eventually pulled over and given citations. Those tickets set recipients back a great deal. They hope to catch up with the next checks, but they never do. Consequently, not only are those men working their butts off, but they are absent from their families for long periods, and since nature abhors a vacuum, before they get their hands on the supposed big, fat checks, they fall for local babes. When their wives find out, things fall apart at home. Your town has helped to contribute to the high rate of divorce in these United States. It has also disproved the notion that more money equals more happiness."

"Sir, I do not know anything about how small cities in Texas make hitherto morally responsible oil-field workers write checks they cannot cover to loose women they hardly know. Please keep the sins of these cities separate. My city may be small, an archenemy of the marriage institution, and stifling by your reckoning, but its police officers, whether young or old, are professionals. They enforce the law without fear or favor. They do all it takes to make sure there are no traffic jams on our roads. You do know that traffic jams impede commerce, right? My city is small, but it is a business-friendly town. That is why its officers make sure to immediately clear scenes of fender-benders before they cause serious accidents and strangle commerce."

"Please, ma'am, stop arguing with me. Get back in the car like I told you to."

"Make me."

"I cannot make you do anything."

"Yes you can. You are like all African men, all-knowing and all-powerful. Your words are law to your women. So make me do your will, master."

"This is America. People here abhor authority figures. We all wear trousers. But your civics lesson for today is that you are now living in the largest city in Texas. Try not to be so fearful. Things do not work here the way they do in your small hometown."

"Well, that is nice to know, but I do not care. I am not going to let you either sweet-talk or strong-arm me into making myself an accessory to anything remotely criminal."

"I am not asking you to commit a crime. Receiving food stamps, veterans benefits, or any government benefit you are not qualified for—those are crimes. I just want you to sit in the car while I run into the courthouse for five minutes. That is not a crime in Texas. It is just stretching a parking ordinance a tiny bit to work for us. Everyone does it."

"Sir, read my lips. I ain't volunteering to be your fall gal, and you can't make me. As they say here in Texas, if you want something done right the first time, do it yourself. That comes directly from the culture of Texas, which has no tolerance for those who try to stretch the laws. So if you feel like stretching them just a tiny bit or a whole lot, you have to do it yourself. Dig?"

As Emmanuel and Mary were arguing, a gentleman who was taking in the debate and appeared amused by it, opened the door to his truck, stepped out, and approached. He seemed to be one of those eternal optimists and compulsive peacemakers dotting the American Midwest. With a broad smile, he extended his hand and said he could have sworn that he had overheard them mention Rig-up City, Texas. They admitted that they had and asked if he was a tow operator. He said that he was not but that their back-and-forth was loud enough to hear even a block away.

The man introduced himself as Bobby Tremble and said he was from Rig-up City. In fact, he had lived there since leaving the military in 1951. He said that as a senior member of the local charitable organization Christians in Action, he was practically a tour guide for that city. He said he was well qualified to field any questions the combative couple might have about his favorite spot in the Permian Basin. Mary quickly corrected him, saying they were not a couple.

"I apologize for my mistake, young lady. You know what they say about assumption—making an ass of you and me, right?"

"That's all right, Bobby. But could you tell this man that he is very wrong about my city?"

"Sir, you are very wrong about Rig-up City, Texas. By the way, what exactly has he got wrong? I know in my wife's estimation, men are always wrong."

"He accused my city of being waterlogged and having a Big Brother law enforcement apparatus designed to impoverish economic refugees and out-of-town motorists. He said Rig-up City is to marriages what Waterloo was to Napoleon Bonaparte, a place to lose it all. He said the allure of making six-figure salaries in the oil fields of the Permian Basin has brought trusting young men to our city, only to undermine their marriages."

"Those are serious indictments, even to a gun-toting, law-and-order kind of guy like me," Bobby said.

"That is what I said, and I am a live-and-let-live' kind of gal," Mary replied gleefully.

"However, when it comes to drainage, he's right," Bobby said. "The city of Houston is nicknamed the Bayou City for a reason. Its runoffs are not absorbed into the ground as quickly as ours are. Therefore, the Bayou City has a leg up on Rig-up City in terms of drainage. But that is not a big deal. It does not rain much in Rig-up City anyway, so it would not make sense to spend the type of money Houston does on a problem that shows up only in leap years in Rig-up City. Having said that let me add that it is ingrained in the culture in my home town to be very frugal even when the economy is humming. We save intuitively. We know that bad times will come, no matter how long the good times last. That is just how it goes in the oil field. Our guest workers do not know that. That is the reason they fall into temptation and literally eat their seed money.

"On the other hand, just like us parents and grandparents, our kids and their kids have money in the bank to weather the inevitable bubbles and busts that constitute the life in the Permian Basin. Most of us buy houses we can afford. I do not have the numbers to show you, but we are the most-frugal of all that the Almighty made in his own image. We have passed on that habit of compulsive saving to our kids. Like I just said, this is not scientific and it's not based on any statistics gathered by the US department of anything, but I guarantee you that despite the enormous wealth my city generates to ease unemployment in this great state, you won't find many of those $300,000 imports cruising down Big Spring Avenue, the main artery connecting Interstate 20 to our downtown. The few you see belong to out-of-town former company-men, who feel the need to show the world they have arrived. We, on the other hand, buy American. We raised our sons and daughters in Ford pickup trucks. They are doing the same thing with their own kids."

"Well, there is a concept in economics propounded by Adam Smith called opportunity cost," Emmanuel said.

"Your children may not be speeding down Main Street in expensive imports, but they participate in other expensive pastimes, like chewing tobacco, smoking tobacco and messing with illegal drugs. They are also spending money covering themselves in expensive tattoos that they call body art. The crime sections of your local papers show your young are downing more adult beverages and encountering the men in blue more than the youths in Houston. But what is your impression of your police officers?"

"In my honest opinion," Bobby said, "they are doing a pretty good job. They may appear to the naked eye to be aggressive, but they are not picking on anyone except drunk drivers. As you can tell, I have been around for a while, so I know this for a fact. Every community does what it has to do to develop programs and the apparatus it needs to maintain peace and order within its confines without violating the civil liberties of those it serves. For instance, every local police department makes traffic rules to get a handle on problems before they become insurmountable mountains.

"Here in Big City, Texas, to reduce accidents on busy Interstate 10 East, eighteen-wheelers are not allowed to enter the left lane until they are safely out of Harris County. Sometimes truckers are in too much of a hurry. Not knowing that it's a setup, they are unwilling to crawl along in the slow-moving right lane. But as soon as they enter the left lane, blue-and-red lights flash behind them. They are pulled over by HPD officers in unmarked pickup trucks. Some of the impatient drivers are found to be from out of town and most likely transporting illegal merchandise to lucrative markets in Louisiana, Alabama, and Georgia. I would not say that the men in blue in your city are being discriminatory that way.

"By the same token, Rig-Up City understands the crucial relationship between time and money. That is why it's making sure that a cordial relationship exists between tractor-trailers, oil-gas equipment transporters, and pickup trucks plying its roads twenty-four hours a day and seven days a week. No one is permitted to muscle out others. Unlike downtown Houston, which has the luxury of being crisscrossed by Loop 610, Highway 288, and Interstates 10, 45, and 59, my city does not have many different routes to get from point A to point B. That is why it cannot let anyone create a bottleneck on its roads. That is why its police seem to be more numerous than they are. They are efficient at keeping traffic moving. They are not into what you call fundraising.

"My businesses have not taken me to all the small cities that make up the Permian Basin. However, I have not spent enough time in these places to develop a negative opinion of their policing. I have heard some people say that officers have been known to follow motorists making their way through town at 3:00 a.m. and to pull them over when the speed changes from 40 mph to 30 mph within the same block. But I have also heard that those officers are business-friendly. If the stickers on the windshield of a motorist's company truck have expired, police will not issue a ticket. The only citation they will give is for speeding. That is friendly."

"Of course, Mr. Bobby, a speeding ticket funnels more money into a city's coffers than an expired sticker citation would," Emmanuel said. "That is the reason they ignore one and not the other."

"On the indictment of our whole area for not being accommodating to marriages, I beg to differ," Bobby said. "I'm not sure how familiar you are with the history of money, but when money was developed, it was not equipped to guard itself. Therefore, those who want to engage in that ubiquitous medium of exchange must provide the security. I do not know what type of relationship you have with money, but I can assure you that if you have lots of money but do not keep a close watch, it will go away without warning. On the other hand, if you do not waste it immediately on what the Good Book calls high living, which I interpret to mean beer and women, your money will grow and will make life easier for you. If you are careful with your money, you and your wife do not have to be in the workforce at the same time and all the days of your life to make ends meet.

"If you do not know it already, know it now. Someone has to be home with the kids, if not all the time, then certainly when they become teenagers and have too much free time, face too many temptations, and take uncalculated risks. It is unfortunate that not all young persons have this path of financial rectitude pointed out to them. That's why they mess up and are not spared the consequences of their ignorance.

"My basic-training sergeant, an extremely mean-spirited pit bull of a man, for no reason used to shout in our faces that we should not only plan on making more money than our dads did after we left the service but also plan on keeping more of what we made. At a time when co-habitation, or shacking-up was unheard of, financial security was the deciding factor when women were considering love, shared pleasure, and marriage. That is one reason I never blew my money. I kept it in a safe place—with my woman. She is a better manager of money than I am. As she would tell you, I am a stronger worker than she is, so I brought home the bacon. My wife stayed home and tended the roost.

"We were always lenders, not borrowers, thank God. She did not visit the casino with whatever money I brought home but did magic with it. She paid our mortgage and our tithe faithfully and thus made us rich materially and spiritually. She kept the house so well that we had no need of a second income. We had enough money saved up for our two boys and one girl to attend and to graduate from

Rig-Up City College. So I know I speak for a majority of my town's folks when I say without hesitation that our home town, where it is not unusual for high school graduates to earn six-figure incomes, has been good for my marriage and for the marriage institution as a whole.

"As for people covering themselves in tattoos, we cannot criminalize that. Some lawyer will tell you that it's a free-speech issue. That is the problem with too much disposable income floating about. In any culture it has emboldened humans to make bad choices. Parents can be a huge help in stemming that tide by teaching their offspring to make the right choices, but when kids have parents who were not themselves taught the fear of the Lord, which King Solomon called the beginning of wisdom, they are at a big disadvantage. As a member of the city council in that nursery rhyme asked when a vicious cat was menacing the local mouse population, who is going to bell the cat?"

"Beats me," Emmanuel said.

"I have another civics lesson for y'all. Do not risk having your automobile towed. There is a county courthouse annex with a drive-through window on Griggs Road. It is not far from here, and there is no waiting. The clerks would be glad to see you. Be well!"

"You too, sir. Thanks, Mr. Bobby," Mary and Emmanuel said in unison.

"Be well, people," he replied.

CHAPTER 4

MARY GOT BACK in the car and buckled up.

"Do you know where Johnston Middle School is located?" she asked.

"Yes, I do," Emmanuel said.

"That is where we are heading," Mary said as she closed her eyes and leaned her head on the head rest. She must have dozed off, because when she opened her eyes and looked up, she found herself staring at the sign for the middle school.

"Sir, I do believe that you have lead foot."

Emmanuel pulled up to the front office to let her out, planning to wait for her in the visitors' parking lot.

"Hold on a second. You are going to do me a big favor."

"Me? You're asking me for help?"

"Yes, I am asking you for help. You can do the happy-dance routine later, but right now, I want you to go with me to meet this monster of a teacher. I do not mean to sound disrespectful and ungrateful, but female teachers seem to have a chip on their shoulders when talking to mothers of their students. Conversely, they seem to be on their best behavior when the parent who shows up for a conference happens to be a man with a chiseled jaw and lots of upper-body muscles."

"That is your perception, but it's distorted because you are looking at things through a defective lens. All teachers by training are professionals."

"Regardless, please go in with me."

Emmanuel and Mary walked into the front office, signed in, and got visitor-passes. They were asked to wait in the outer office for the teacher they were there to see. But before they could get comfortable in their chairs, she appeared and shepherded them to her classroom, six portable buildings away. Inside, students were busy. They seemed to be involved in group projects. The teacher pulled up chairs for Emmanuel and Mary.

"Can we make this real quick?" Mary asked. "I have to go back to work."

"Sure," the teacher said. She asked Mary if it was okay to invite the child about whom the teacher-conference was about, and Mary said it was. The teacher signaled Amy to come to her desk. When she got there, the teacher went straight to her concerns.

"Your child has been disrespectful, not just to me but to guest teachers. She is very disruptive and seems to want to take over my class."

"No, ma'am, my child is a good kid—a model kid, in fact. I taught her good manners. She knows not to get out of line. Don't you, dear?"

"Yes, Momma."

"See? I know that I raised my child right."

"Please understand that I am not saying she is not a good kid or has not been raised right. If anything, she is just being a kid. However, this being a learning environment, I insist on King Solomon's rule stipulating that there is a proper time for everything. There is a time to play, and certainly for every child, there is time to build a foundation for the future. Your child and her friends are disruptive and disrespectful. Even after being admonished, they will not stop talking while I am trying to teach. It gets worse when I am not here. One day when she was asked to turn in her homework your child angrily stood up as if she was going to assault the substitute teacher. She told him, 'I got no freaking homework to turn in. What are you going to do about it?' Your child makes my helpers spend valuable time writing incident reports rather than teaching my students. That should not be the case. No learning goes on when teachers are burdened with writing incident reports. That is the wrong use of class time. It benefits nobody."

"Excuse me, miss. May I say something?" Emmanuel tried to add his voice to the discussion, but Mary would not let him.

"Maybe your lessons are boring the kids," Mary said. "Spice them up a little bit and you will have their undivided attention. Kids these days need to be stimulated. Every teacher with a passing knowledge of child psychology knows that, but do you?"

"I will let the Texas Department of Education worry about my qualifications to teach sixth grade. I am just a teacher, not an administrator. But I do know that out of hundreds of candidates who applied for this position, I was offered the job. Though I readily admit I don't know a whole lot about psychology, I love my job and I love and care about the children in my classroom. Your child, however, does not appear to care about being educated. She has been bringing family photographs instead of completed homework to class.

She passed photos around even when I was making eye contact with her. She refused to retrieve them when I asked her to do so. I told her I was going to report her to you. She said it would be a waste of my time because she was sure you would be too busy to take the call. The day I called you was the third one on which she gave me the excuse that she forgot her homework and would bring it the next day. We cannot have that. Homework must be turned in when due. That is the school district's policy, not mine. This is not a battle for teachers only. Parents have to help on the home front."

"Please help us, miss," Emmanuel pleaded.

"Okay, but you must help me. Teachers can succeed in opening minds to knowledge only if parents provide boundaries and stability and guide their children at home. The term *super teacher* is a misnomer. Teachers cannot do it all."

"Miss, can I make a suggestion?"

"Yes, sir."

"I am not trying to tell you how to run your classroom, but is there any way you could rearrange it so this child is separated from her group? I think that if the gang is broken up, most likely it will no longer have the power to take over your class."

"Thank you. That is an excellent suggestion. But as I said, no matter what tweaking we do in the eight hours we have your child with us, you as her parents have to do your part when she is at home. Teach her respect for others and for herself. I suggest that you limit her association with a particular girl. That other child seems to be the leader of the group, and your child, who is far smarter than all the others, tries to imitate that leader. I tried to separate them, but that other child said it was not her fault that your daughter looked up to her. She had a point. That is the reason I also invited her parents to see me while you are here on campus."

At that moment, someone from the office paged the teacher, saying another set of parents were waiting for her at the main office. She excused herself and went to meet them.

When the teacher returned, she introduced the adults to each other. She told the new arrivals about the problems involving their child. She asked them if it was okay to invite their child to join the adults. They gave their consent, and the teacher beckoned Melody to approach. She did and immediately began to vigorously defend herself, shedding oceans of tears in the process.

"I would be minding my own business, and she would come over to talk about Jermaine," the girl said, pointing toward Mary's daughter.

"We do not have a Jermaine in my classroom. Who is Jermaine?" the teacher asked.

"Jermaine is a boy she wants to go with."

"What?" Mary blurted out.

"Which Jermaine are we talking about?" Melody's mom asked.

"Our Jermaine, your nephew."

"Oh no!"

"What do you mean by that, ma'am?" the teacher asked.

"Well, if Jermaine is my sister's child, we've got a huge problem. My nephew has been nothing but trouble in middle school. As a last resort, the authorities sent him to an alternative school, but sometimes it takes the police to get him there. Not only is he a bad kid, but he does not seem to care about the consequences. He delights in shocking people by saying that he needs an education only so he can count his money, because when he grows up, he wants to be a big drug dealer."

Mary was so shocked, humiliated, and upset that she jumped up to choke her daughter, but the other adults would not let her.

"Have you been doing exactly what I have been warning you not to do and neglecting your schoolwork? I told you that education was a time-sensitive commodity and that romance would have to wait until you are grown up. You have seen what happened to me. I did not wait and I am paying a heavy price for it. As my father said, I was in too much of a hurry and put the cart in front of the horse. Now look at me not too many years later. I am paying for my foolishness with high blood pressure, diabetes, and joint pains. These problems came to me not by way of advanced age as they did with my grandmother. No, mine resulted from standing on my feet for too many hours in dead-end jobs, and yet I cannot even afford the luxury of living from paycheck to paycheck. Why would you wish all that on yourself?"

Mary was so upset that she called her supervisor to get permission to take the rest of the day off. She intended not just to cool off at home but to search for a leather belt with which to give her daughter the whipping of her life when she got home. The request was denied. The nurse in charge said Mary had to get back to work immediately.

Emmanuel ran Mary back to her job.

Mary went up to her work floor and swiped her time card on a machine mounted on a wall in the break room.

The supervising nurse was waiting right outside the room to hand Mary a list of chores needing immediate attention. She ignored the woman and instead went to the restroom. After waiting for a while at the nurses' station for Mary to come out, the supervising nurse sent a nurse aide to the bathroom to find out what was keeping Mary. The aide found Mary on the floor, weeping. The aide rushed out and alerted her boss that Mary seemed to be experiencing a crisis and looked suicidal.

The nurse raced into the bathroom where she saw Mary sitting on the floor, talking to herself. The supervisor ran back to her station and paged another registered nurse, asking her to come ASAP. When that nurse arrived, the supervising nurse asked her to watch over the floor and rushed back into the bathroom.

"Talk to me. Are you all right, Mary?"

"Why does everyone keep asking me that?"

"Because you are not acting normally. Are you sure that you are all right?"

"Yes, I am all right. Why do you keeping asking me that? Of course I am all right."

"You could have fooled me. What's going on with you? You say you are fine, but at the same time you shake your head as if to say you are not. You cannot be all right if you are sitting on the floor of a hospital bathroom, tears running down your face. The rumor mill here has it that you got no man in your life, so who is breaking your heart? Are you having suicidal thoughts?"

"Of course I am having thoughts of killing myself. What else is there for me? My thirteen-year-old has added exponentially to my enormous burden. She is turning out to be just like me in the very worst way."

"What do you mean by that?"

"My daughter is trying to be the sad echo of me when I was her age. She is happily running down the same dangerous avenue that led me to a permanent state of unhappiness and chronic depression."

"What is the surprise there? Kids are designed to take after their parents. About 70 percent of them choose to copy their mamas over their daddies. That is settled science, but it seems to have spooked you terribly. Why? What has your daughter gotten her-self into? What new youthful indiscretion has she discovered?"

"The same mess I delighted in right before I became a newly minted teenager."

"That is nothing new. Do not choose death because of it. But how big is the mess we are talking about?"

"It is a very serious one."

"When did you find out that she was diving into a cesspool?"

"This afternoon when I called in, I was at the school. Her teacher had called to tell me that my daughter and another child were holding her class for ransom. I went up there with a friend. The other child, very articulate, pointed out that my daughter was the problem. I told her and her parents that my child was a straight-A student enrolled in a program for gifted students and that in the last school year she had won the district's Dr. Martin Luther King 'I Have a Dream' essay contest. I said my child belongs to a group of self-motivated students so focused on their studies that they have no time to be disruptive in school. I said my daughter is so busy that she does not have time to get in trouble. I demanded to know who put that classmate up to smearing my child and what she would gain after getting my child in trouble.

"That child responded as coolly and as seriously as if she were reading from a court document. She said that I could be right about all of my child's accomplishments but that among her peers on campus my child was not considered the angel I held her out to be. On the contrary, that child told me, my daughter was accumulating street credentials by projecting a bad image to impress boys whom she hoped to run away with in the immediate future. That little urchin challenged me to ask any of her fellow students if the image of my child that I projected jibed with the image of her that they knew. Against the advice of the teacher and of the girl's parents, I asked that child to bring it on.

"The teacher said it was a bad idea, but I refused to be persuaded. Each of the children asked to come up to the teacher's desk described a child set on self-destruction. That sounded familiar."

"What do you mean?"

"That was the same trap I had set for myself at about the age my daughter is right now. I managed to fall through the cracks despite living under the same roof with both parents. I wanted to do what felt good. My parents were caring people. They wanted nothing but the best for me. But my plans were different."

"Come on! Not you. I can't imagine you sporting pink-and-purple hair with one side of your head shaved bald or wearing only black clothing as I used to do in an effort to convince the world that I was a punk-rocker."

"As they say, appearances can be deceiving. I may look like the mother-superior of some convent now, but I used to hate straight-laced boys. Though I did not smoke, I liked boys who smoked a little bit of marijuana, wore do-rags, got tattoos, and regularly cut school. Boys from good families were offensive to me and to my agenda. I wanted to be a rebel. Therefore, I admired the borderline lawbreakers, if not the complete outlaw types, the thugs. The more these boys refused to conform to adult expectations, the more I desired them. Even when it became clear that they were the ones most scared of committed relationships, I still craved them."

"You and I seem to have been cut from the same cloth. We went out of our way to get into trouble for boys who did not give a damn about us, their female dogs. But for a combination of luck, the grace of God, and the efforts of concerned pastors, I could not have survived my own excesses."

"I heard that," Mary said. "In my case, I know now that my excesses were responsible for the untimely death of my parents' harmonious marriage. Dad had observed me and had seen the destructive direction I was taking. He sprang into action and did everything he could to save me from myself. He blocked every avenue that might lead to my destruction. He tried to recruit my mom to fortify the defense. Mom and her friends good-naturedly pooh-poohed him and told him to relax. Dad did not think this was a laughing matter, but he was a smart man. He did not want to start an argument with his woman, but he made up his mind to disband what he called the Vanity Fair.

"We used to have a successful bake-shop owner in my neighborhood. His nickname was I-Bros. He was disgusted with the statistics showing that America had the highest incidence of teenage motherhood in the Western Hemisphere—fifty-two per thousand compared with Great Britain's thirty-two per thousand. He felt that something should be done about the statistic. He discussed the problem with friends and business associates. He tried to keep his daughter pure in the hope that she wouldn't contribute to that number. He hired a domestic staff that included a chauffeur for the child while she was still in junior high. But despite the fences, moats, and strongholds those people erected, that child found a crack and fell through it. To add insult to injury, she had no idea who the father of her baby was.

"My dad carefully analyzed the I-Bros girl's situation and reached two conclusions. One was that the girl used to dress too scandalously for a community where liquor stores were never open on Sundays. The other was that a good dad had no business outsourcing the supervision of his potentially trampy daughter to paid helpers. Dad decided to show the world how the problem of young girls doing all they can to fail the parents should be tackled. But just to be sure, he consulted with Mr. Mayfield, who told him that the manner of dressing was nothing more than a cover. The problem, he said, was actually biological and had to be handled with tact and care."

"Who was Mr. Mayfield?"

"He was a schoolteacher, the most giving and respected person in our community when we were growing up. He was popular because he was generous with his time and because he and his wife shared the okra, kale, watermelons, blueberries, and spinach they grew in the backyard of their beautiful home in the summer."

"The man may have been a deacon," the nurse suggested. "Deacons get their marching orders to be community-oriented people directly from the Good Book. They and their families are required to live giving, peaceful lives free of scandal. That may have been the reason he was in your dad's men's fellowship."

"You mean the men's fellowship, as in church?"

"Yes. My grandfather used to belong to one."

"There was no men's fellowship for my dad. At that point, he was a borderline atheist who spent a great deal of his time looking for ways to discredit God, faulting him for man-made disasters like the overpopulation in India, the endemic poverty in Haiti, and man's inhumanity to his fellow man across Africa."

"How did he explain himself?"

"What do you mean?"

"Your dad grew up in the Deep South, also known as the Bible Belt, correct?"

"That is correct."

"Are you saying that he was not affiliated with any church at a point in the history of the United States when houses of worship were regarded as places of comfort for those marginalized by the larger society because of their skin color?"

"My father did not do church except for life events like christenings, weddings, and funerals to which he was invited by name. But when it came to barbecue, his fellow Masons cited my dad as turning out the best in Texas.

At that time in our little country town, the top venue for wedding receptions and other formal occasions was a banquet hall owned by Daddy's fraternal order. And that was where my dad used to wow people with his cooking. I guess you could say that the barbecue pit was where he and Mr. Mayfield made each other's acquaintance."

"So I suppose that when your dad suspected your biology was pushing you to butt heads with him, he ran to Mr. Mayfield for help to avoid a collision."

"Basically, yes. He paired me with one of his boys."

"But the emergency pairing with a Mayfield boy did not end up in marriage. Why?"

"The man had taught his kids to think and to act like adults. No fooling around. He trusted them. They trusted him. They did not like to sneak around to do something I wanted to do if it would displease their dad. Not much excited them. I could not stand them. Their father controlled them like puppets. The man even controlled his wife. My mom and her friends thought he was a first-class control freak. I felt called to liberate that family. But now as the parent of a child who is as crazy as I was back then, I see what the man was trying to do."

"That's right. There is nothing like parenthood to make you think like a parent. But did you or your mom ever hear Mrs. Mayfield complain about the second-class status assigned to her by that evil husband of hers?"

"No, my mother and her friends were secretly jealous of what Mrs. Mayfield had."

"They were? Why?"

"They thought she had it made. She did not have to work. She held no job outside of the home. My mom's friends had to work. Sometimes they even worked overtime. They hated every minute of it, but being ardent feminists, they would not admit that to outsiders. Mrs. Mayfield was a stay-at-home mom, a status most of those women secretly coveted. To the activists among my mother's contemporaries, Mr. Mayfield was a villain. In their estimation, her husband had denied her the chance to be her own person. They thought she could break out of that prison with their help. Mrs. Mayfield was sympathetic to these women, but she absolutely refused to be recruited as a foot soldier in their fight. Neither would she permit her household to be used as a staging ground for the battle of the sexes. In her estimation, whatever quality in her husband that the activists found offensive had worked for her. Her kids were excelling in their studies. They were never in trouble in school or outside of school."

"The militants seemed to have had a point, but given the success of all the Mayfield kids, I agree with Mrs. Mayfield that her man was a genius in letting her tend the roost while he was out hunting down the bacon. My grandmother used to tell my mom that if more families decided to do that, county jails would be repurposed into college lecture rooms and housing."

"Sister, your granny was so right. But to my dad's eternal disappointment, I lacked the good sense to know that he was looking toward the future. That future in the case of the Mayfield boys was already mapped out by their father in the blueprint given to their mom as the executor of his estate. But as I said, my inclination was toward the boys with no values. I always admired thugs. The more anti-parent and anti-establishment they were, the more I was attracted to them. I wanted no part of clean-cut boys. I found no excitement in them. I expected that feeling to be fully mutual."

"I always wanted to be a spiky-haired, dark, angry bad girl. How cool is that? You and I were in the same sisterhood without knowing each other. It is safe to say that I did all the bad things you did. But I left no scandalous trail behind me because no parent was probing my daily activities and my whereabouts with a fine-tooth comb. I guess I was lucky in not having a parent watching over me and expecting me to get a scholarship to an Ivy League college. My mom worked menial jobs. She rode the bus and usually arrived home late and very tired. Those circumstances, plus the fact that she was struggling with her personal life—she could not keep a man—forced her to be not just my trusted friend but an eternal optimist who believed I would do the right thing, parenting myself."

"When my dad was being charitable to parents like your mom, he used to say that such parents mistook their little darlings for thinking people."

"As a parent now, I agree with that assessment but with an exception. In defense of my mom, I think she made a healthy choice. Like her, though I did not know what I was doing, I was set on doing it anyway. So if she had to worry about what I was doing when she was desperate to find a man she could call her own, she would have had a nervous breakdown."

"So it is true that what you do not know won't hurt you?"

"Yes, ignorance is sometimes bliss, but Mom was not totally clueless and unconcerned about my running around on the streets. She just believed that I would be careful not to get too hurt. Maybe, as you said, that made her an astute enabler. That was okay. She did not have enough education to shake her belief that kids should be allowed to make mistakes. She thought that if their experimentation did not kill them, they would become stronger. Therefore, if someone had told my mom that while other kids were working on getting their driving permits, I was working hard on losing my virginity to very bad boys, she would have posited that since I did not have a dad in my life, I was merely reaching out to those who represented a father figure to me. No harm done."

"I am jealous. Your mom was totally cool."

"You can say that again! But that coolness brought about head-on collisions with her parents, who are in their seventies and still married and continue to cherish each other. Till this day, they hold hands as they used to do long ago."

"When old folks hold hands, it's not necessarily a function of affection. It may have to do with leaning on each other for support."

"That may be true and might be an even better reason. They say that we humans thrive when we are afforded emotional, physical, and spiritual support. They were very opposed to the way my mom ran her life and were disappointed that she did not emulate them like their other children did."

"Are you saying that her siblings turned out differently?"

"They did and are still happily married. They still say that my mom has a boyfriend-addiction issue. They say that she found her men at bars, made babies with them, and moved on. My dad is the only man she could stand long enough to marry. They made me and my twin siblings. My granny said my mother divorced my father because he tried to rein her in by putting a stop to her clubbing and gambling. She told him they were not compatible. She told him to move on, because she was a free spirit and he was not."

"Was your dad controlling?"

"No he was not. My grand-parents loved that man so much they pleaded with the court to give our custody to him. The court did the usual thing; gave my mom custody. Dad paid her child-support, but after mom dumped us much of the time with him and ran to the casinos in Louisiana her parents went to court and asked it to reverse itself. It did, but Mom never got around to paying the man the child-support she told the court she would. He never asked her. He never complained."

"As I told you, I had an interventionist dad. My mom was all right, but your mom was the type of mother every free-spirited girl dreams about. But given that she was an enabler to a fault, how did you end up a success?"

"Well, I had my epiphany, though it was not because I was in search of it. Something called grace came to me. It was accompanied by luck, another phenomenon outside the control of humans. Though it was unintended, it was an unmistakable second chance to reinvent myself. As my mother's mother would say, I was able to put new wine into a new wineskin."

"How could anyone meaningfully reinvent himself or herself?"

"There is a single-cell organism called luck unrecognized by science. Hard work has been suspected to increase the propensity for this phenomenon, but luck for the most part is just luck. It is not something you earn. It is a byproduct of grace."

"You sound like my mom when she was trying to get my dad to overlook one of my deliberate infractions of his house rules."

"Thanks. One summer day, my bad boy and I were at a park, intensely making out. We were quite graphic. I later learned that parents felt the need to cover the eyes of their kids as they were passing by the park bench my bad boy had commandeered for us.

"At that time, my mom, having failed to find her dream man—a man in his late thirties without kids—at singles bars, clubs, dating agencies, or at work, decided for a short time to leave her affairs in the hands of a higher authority. She took us and her search to a church.

"On that balmy summer day, unbeknown to me, my mother's pastor, to whom I was never introduced, was at the park to coach a Little League team. He recognized me on account of my cute face, which looked like my mom's. I still have no idea how that man could have recognized me when my guy and I were so completely intertwined with each other that we looked like a pretzel.

"The pastor had waited patiently. When we came up for air like deep-sea divers who had been at the bottom of the ocean, he tapped me on the shoulder to let me know where I was.

"He asked me point blank if I knew that I was selling myself cheaply in a public arena to someone who obviously did not care about me, my future, or my reputation. He said that even if I did not care about my reputation, I needed to know that I was setting a bad example for innocent youths, mostly grade schoolers, who were out that evening with their dads, their moms, and other relatives to learn the rudiments of baseball and football.

"My guy would not let me answer that intrusive question. He told the pastor that I was not a public figure like a movie star or a sports hero. Consequently, I had neither the expectation nor the moral obligation to be held up as a role model for children. That was the sole domain of parents, he said. My guy also told the pastor that he indeed cared about me. The pastor pointed out to him that I was practically naked. He said no boy who cared about a girl would want to see her in a compromising position, especially in a public setting.

My guy stood up for me again. He pointed out to the pastor that my dad was no good. He added that since the pastor held himself out to be a good man, a claim my father could not possibly make, the pastor could not be my dad. Since he did not qualify as a dad to me, my guy said, he had no right to limit my freedom of expression and of association, a gross violation of the Constitution. I was impressed. Even the pastor was impressed. He conceded that my guy sounded like an academic. He said that my guy had a future as a US Supreme Court justice. All I had to do, the pastor added, was to get him through high school by any means necessary. My guy warned him not to try to play dad to him.

"The pastor said that real men treat the bodies of their women as sacred temples. Consequently, he said, no man who cared about his woman would make a public exhibit of her the way mine was doing. Real men, he said, would not strip their valuable possessions of clothing and of human dignity like mine had done. The pastor said that what I was letting my guy do to me was a public exhibition that even a decently paid prostitute would find offensive. My guy responded that the pastor was an old man set in the past who did not know that we lived in a modern era when less clothing was in and too much clothing was out.

"'Preacher man,' he said, 'I take it that you're not a married man. Either that or you have never attended modern marriage counseling classes. If you had, you would have learned that public displays of affection, particularly by the young, are beneficial to society, assisting nature in perpetuating the human species.'

"The pastor responded that he was not in school the semester that course was offered at the marital academy. But looking me in the eye, he asked: Who was the beneficiary of the *laissez les bon temps rouler?* I said I did not know what language that was. He said he was not surprised, given that I was not getting anything out of being so shamelessly exhibited in public. He said my guy, who was fully clothed and was benefiting from having me make a public spectacle of myself, knew what the popular French saying meant. My guy thought about that for a second. Then he asked the pastor if he knew we were in a committed relationship. The pastor replied that he had been out of town lately and therefore was not privy to that news but would like to be brought up to date on the quality of the commitment. When my guy hesitated, the pastor went on.

"'You would excuse me, won't you young man? On account of the humidity, my glasses are a little bit foggy today, so I could be wrong about this, but I do not seem to see your ring on this child's finger. Do you? Or is your signet of the invisible variety?' That question made me involuntarily survey my fingers. 'Why are you showing uncertainty?' the pastor asked us. My guy said that a ring was nothing but a piece of metal and that in any case we did not owe him an explanation as to whether rings had been exchanged. The pastor said a ring might well be a piece of cheap, man-made material but had for eternity symbolized the joining of two hearts in an unbroken circle of commitment.

My guy seemed uncomfortable with that logic. He got angrier. He said he did not want to put his hands on an old man but would if the pastor did not mind his own business and take a hike. The man eyeballed me again and pointing to my exposed breasts said emphatically that my guy was a player of the worst sort and that at any place two or three humans were gathered, I would be considered a fool for not recognizing that. He said that given the fact I was not a toy, I had no good reason to allow myself to be passed around and played like a soccer ball.

"'Old man, how do you know I am a player if you are not one yourself?' my guy demanded. He got in the pastor's face and told him it was not true that wisdom came with age. He said if that were the case, the pastor would have known that youthful adventures and the mistakes that come with them often resulted in mature self-discovery.

"'I agree that this child is making a big mistake," the pastor said. "As for you, what you are doing to this child and others like her are not a mistake. It is a deliberate act of evil for which hellfire awaits you.'

"My guy ordered the pastor to buzz off with a parting shot, saying I was his wife-to-be. Me? Did my guy just refer to me as a wife-to-be? I had never heard a sweeter phrase in all my life. I was so euphoric that I did not hear or care about what the pastor was saying to me after that. He was not making sense. The man was trying to shame me into doing what he considered moral. He failed. My guy pulled me to my feet from the park bench as I struggled to pull up my zipper.

"'Are you sure you are a man of the cloth?' my guy asked.

"'Yes, I am. That I am sure of,' the pastor responded.

"My guy fired back, 'Then how come you do not know that meddling in the business of others will not work? According to your own manual, many waters can't quench love. Neither can floods. If love is that strong—even stronger than death, the book says—what makes you think you can stop my girl from being with me?'

"'Are we looking at a master/slave relationship here? I believe I heard you use what in English grammar is called a possessive pronoun, but I have not heard you say that you love her, that you love this possession of yours. Do you?'

"'It does not matter.'

"'What you are dangling in the face of this child to hypnotize her does not qualify as love. It does not meet even the most watered-down definition of love, but it is okay with you for her to think love is what you are offering. The correct term is exploitation. And that is wrong because you know you are conning her. She does not know that yet. She is too trusting to know that. Why don't you be a real man and level with her that your scheme is to use her body for your pleasure and then to discard it in some out-of-the-way place? Why don't you tell her that she is running with the devil and that he's not her friend? You do not want to lose her. That's why. You are so right. I can't stop you. As a matter of fact, nothing can stop your trail of destruction. Nothing can stop you from bulldozing and plundering this child, not when she is a willing victim of your forked-tongue. But all I want you to do is level with her. Stop being a wolf in a sheep's clothing.'

"At that point, my guy made a fist and waved it in front of the pastor. 'Preacher man, do not let me deploy this weapon of mass destruction on you. I know you do not have a health insurance. Even if you do, it will not be enough to put you back together after I am through with you. You are already in bad shape. Your body does not store oxygen anymore. So take your moral policing somewhere else before you get hurt.' He got so close to the unflinching pastor that the man could feel my guy's breath on his face.

"'Preacher man, I want so you so bad I can smell your blood,' my guy said.

"It looked to me like the pastor was aware of his mortality.

"'Heal,' the pastor said and stepped back from my guy. That flinch gave my guy a newfound boldness.

"'Watch this, preacher man,' my guy said as he surprised even me by plunging a hand inside the waistband of my underwear and pulling me to himself.

"The pastor commented that it was just like a dog lifting a hind leg on every tree and fire hydrant it comes across.

"'We see pit bulls doing that all the time,' the pastor said. 'In science, it is called marking the territory. A dog's marking does not constitute a title transfer of the territory marked. Therefore, your markings do not convey ownership,' he told my guy.

"My guy told him that there was a reason the United States had neither a king nor a moral police agency in its more than two hundred years of existence.

"I was so happy to be liberated from that man that I sucked on my guy's lips to show my defiance. We went around the corner. My guy decided that we needed to celebrate our victory over the preacher man right away. So he quickly got us a room since I had to be home before my granny got there to give me lunch money and school supplies.

"As we were sharing pleasure, there was a knock on the door. I thought someone had made a mistake since I had dutifully hung a 'Do Not Disturb' sign on the door. I asked my guy to ignore the knock and to concentrate on me and what we were doing, but he got up immediately and opened the door without asking me if it was okay and without caring whether I was decent or not. As I pulled the comforter over me, several guys, two of them lugging cases of imported beer, stepped into the room and locked the dead bolt on the door. They all reeked of weed. I asked what they were doing in the room when we were having what in most cultures and religions, is a personal and private. My guy didn't answer. One guy sat on the dresser, one sat on the other twin bed, and two sat on the bed I was lying on and removed their shoes. I asked my guy again what his friends were doing there. No one answered my question. Instead, they pulled down their pants. I protested when my guy pulled the comforter off of me.

"My guy calmly explained that just as a pudding is tested in eating it, his home boys were there for me to prove I loved him as much as I had been telling him. I mentioned the heart pendant I had bought him for Valentine's Day and the expensive red tennis shoes I had gotten him for his birthday. I recalled how I had been skipping lunch to make my meal money available to him to buy an expensive guitar he'd been dying to have, plus the numerous times I had forgiven him after I caught him kissing other girls while we were supposed to be going steady. He answered that those things were important landmarks in any relationship but not perfect indicators of my fidelity to him. I did not understand that logic. My facial expression betrayed me. I was never good at thinking on my feet, how much more when I was on my back. I looked lost, so he explained his expectations again.

"I argued that what he wanted to share with his friends was supposed to be exclusive to us. He said he agreed. I tried to make him see that I was not communal property readily available to his buddies. I told him my body was my most prized possession, which, as the pastor had hinted, would be greatly devalued if his friends were welcome to partake of it. My guy answered that not only would the gold remain intact if I complied with him, but the participation by his friends would make the bond between us grow even stronger. I tried to think of something sensible to say, but with his eyes trained on me, my mind had no clarity. 'I was going to ask you to remember how I stood up for you when it mattered, but I see that preacher man has already turned you against me,' he said. I told him that was not the case. He said it was. To prove I was not aligning myself with the pastor, I went along with what my guy called 'inclusion.'

"The things we do when we believe we're being offered love!" Mary said.

"What about your self-discovery? When did your light-bulb moment come?"

"I never arrived at that moment. I kept going and going like a dry cell powered by the sun. I am the example that some experts cite to buttress their claim that the success of a child does not depend on the marital status of the parents. That is the reason I fear for my daughter. Like her, I was strongly attracted to all types of troubles. I wanted to be nothing but a bad girl. I had no idea what I would gain from it, but I wanted to be a piece of trash. To me, success meant being a sort of training wheel, available to every boy who wanted to experiment."

"Did you not say that your dad and Mr. Mayfield had a plan to counter that tendency? They assigned you a boy, right?"

"Yes. But the truth is that this choirboy made things worse for me. He pushed me to extreme badness."

"How did he do that?"

"That boy's wholesome, pristine image goaded me into being even worse than I set out to be. Being around him was so suffocating that I sometimes felt like using his ever-present necktie to strangle him. Even when his dad was not watching us, the kid insisted on acting in what he considered a moral, ethical way, doing only the things his dad would permit. What young person did you know who wanted to live like that, particularly at the age when exploring and shopping around were a rite of passage?"

"Oh, I used to know a bunch of boys like that. They were raised by nuns. But your designated future husband was raised by parents just like yours. You should have found common ground in that."

"The Mayfield kid's parents turned him into an altar boy. They did a very bad job. He was too straight-laced. He was raised to be feeble-minded and dependent on his parents. Though he could drive, he would have his dad drop us off at the cinema. Most sane boys would have welcomed the opportunity to get behind the wheel with a beautiful girl like me. They also would have welcomed the darkness of the theater, seizing the chance to make out, but my assigned boyfriend would not even hold my hand."

"I guess that ruled out kissing."

"One time I tried to kiss him, but he stopped me and said, 'Not prudent. Dad would not approve of that.' He lacked the self-confidence to be his own person. Meanwhile, my friends were telling me how they were making out with boys at every opportunity. Some of them even went all the way. Me? I could not get this guy to sit and have a conversation. That was so unfair. The more I tried to be his woman, the more he tried to avoid being left alone with me. He was very weird."

"You know some kids are not like you and I were. They take very seriously the injunction that children should obey their parents un-conditionally."

"What other young man did you know who bought his girl a bouquet of flowers on a non-prom night?"

"I hate to say it, but it's not entirely wrong for a boy to bring his date flowers. This practice is not intended for prom nights only. Neither is it an indicator of old age. All well-mannered, cultured men bring flowers to their dates. It is a Western-cultural tradition that shows sophistication."

"My dad was an avid gun collector. He never tired of showing off his collection even to total strangers. He was also known to sometimes display a bad temper when my mom and Mr. Mayfield were not around. Word spread quickly that he would fire one of his weapons at any boy who got too close to me. But there was one boy who did not get the memo or who thought I was worth the risk. One day, as usual, I was dressed very provocatively. In a chance encounter at the water fountain, he said I was very hot and whispered an indecent proposal to me. It sounded like he could not wait to make a woman out of me. I smiled my encouragement. He flashed a victory sign at me and walked away. I immediately decided he was my type of guy.

"Not long after, my family was having picnic at a park, and the boy sighted me. There was no water fountain where we could meet. I was ecstatic to see him but hoped he would not stop by. However, he did. This boy did not meet the standard of refinement my dad had set for young men. He wore shorts and a sleeveless shirt, which exposed all his tattoos. His hair cried out for soap and water.

"We had more than enough food. My dad, who was never stingy with food, fixed the boy a plate, as he did for everyone who passed by. The boy took that to mean he was family. He tried to sit by me. I admired his boldness, his take-charge attitude. But Dad wouldn't let him sit anywhere. He could hardly stand being in the same county with him. The boy sized up Dad, turned around, and tried to talk to me. That was when Dad asked him to leave. 'All right, calm down, old man!' he said as Dad took a few steps toward him. Dad warned him not to try to contact me, but the boy did not get it.

"He said to me, '*Yo te llamare mañana.*' In Spanish that means 'I will call you tomorrow.' '*Llama me, por favor,*' I responded.

"'No, he won't call,' my dad said. He had always thought I was up to no good, but from that day forward, he would not let me out of his sight. Though Mom had paid for my driver education, he drove me everywhere I needed to go. I became the laughingstock of my friends.

"One day the United Negro College Fund and girls from the local chapter of the Sigma Gamma Rho sorority set up a booth at the Urban League to talk to young girls about college and finances. Other parents brought their kids at seven in the morning and came back for them after 2:00 p.m. My dad did not do as those parents did. He stayed the whole day, looking bored and tired. But when he took me to the library, he never came inside with me. Maybe he thought the librarians were on his side in the fight to keep me a virgin. He would drop me off, run a few errands, and then return to pick me up. That was like leaving the barn door open and expecting the cattle to stay put. The boy who had been warned to stay away from me soon learned of this opportunity. We met at the library at least once a week to map out a plan for carrying out his indecent proposal.

"We could have continued using the library as a rendezvous point forever, but his bad-boy image, which I liked so much, made that impossible. My guy had a permanent angry look about him, and he was loud, a bad fit for a venue where patrons demanded quiet. He relished getting into people's faces and let everyone know he was not a gentleman and should not be expected to hold doors for little old ladies. All that brashness caught up with him.

Older library patrons who knew me were concerned and told my father that one day soon he would be asked to come down to the police station to bail me out—or to visit the morgue to identify my body. After that alert, Dad would bring me to the library and waited, reading magazines. Sometimes he sat with me until I finished what I needed to do. Whenever Dad sat with me, the boy knew to stay away. Unable to be with me, he stopped coming. I lost interest in the library when that happened.

"But then came the weekend leading to the celebration of Dr. Martin Luther King Jr.'s birthday. That was my big chance before winter set in, and I could no longer use school activities as an excuse to escape Dad's hawk-like supervision. Several civic groups assembled to recognize local kids who had done exceptionally well in school. Everyone from grade schoolers to national politicians gave speeches at this huge event. Dad manned the barbecue pits as usual and was enjoying the adulation of the fans of his cooking. Suddenly the chaplain complained that the sound system had quit on him. Dad went inside the hall and within minutes found that the young disc jockey had pumped up the music so high that he had fried the amp. Since Dad never trusted anyone else with his grills, he would not abandon his post to dash back to our house for a replacement sound system. He asked Mom to take me home to fetch one of our amplifiers.

Away from Dad's sight, Mom handed me the keys to her car and told me to be careful. My bad boy must have been watching from a distance. I went around the corner and stopped at a stop sign, and he dove in. Almost immediately he complained that we did not have the time for me to be driving so slowly. I moved over and let him take the helm. He stepped on the gas and turned my mom's Mark VII into a land jet. Dad had bought that car for Mom because it was comfortable to ride, but I never knew it was designed for speed too. Within minutes, we pulled into my carport. I unlocked the door and we got on the couch.

"It did not seem to us that we had been gone for long. Apparently we had. The gathering at the banquet hall was still missing a sound system, and Dad was expected to solve the problem. Suspecting that I was having difficulties disconnecting the amp from the rest of his sound system, he came home to help me.

"I did not hear Dad unlock the door. Or perhaps we were in such a hurry that we had not bothered to close and lock it. When Dad entered the living room he lifted the boy off of me and threw him across the room like professional wrestlers do their scrawny opponents. Then Dad turned to me. He showed no mercy. He yanked the cushion from under me and I fell to the floor. He kicked me like a football. I struggled up. He whipped me all over my body with a leather belt as I stood up on one foot, trying to put on my pants. I fell on the floor in the process. That gave him a wider surface to inflict pain. As the whip left its mark on my bare back and buttocks, I regretted rejecting my mom's advice that morning to put on a dress instead of a pair of jeans which made me look like I was poured into them.

"When Dad turned to ask my lover what he was doing in our house, I grabbed my clothes and ran out the door; very naked, yet unconcerned whether neighbors and passersby would appreciate the exhibit or consider it indecent exposure.

I expected my partner to flee with me, but from outside, I could see that my bad boy was not very smart. Either that or I was so carried away by my expectation of being made a woman that I failed him. I didn't mention to him that not only was my father an excellent nose tackle during his high school years but that because of his quickness, he was a much-sought-after sparring partner for many of the top pugilists of his day."

"Your bad boy was dumb? Why do you say that about a boy you were doing just about anything to be with?"

"I saw him standing up to my father instead of following my example and escaping the lion's den the way I did—naked."

"Was your guy bigger than your dad, leading him to assume he could take the man in his own house?"

"No, that is the reason I characterized him the way I did. My bad boy was dumb as a nail. I kept hollering at the top of my lungs for him to run. He did not have to prove anything to Dad. I was the only one he should have tried to impress, and I already knew what he could do."

"How much did the mistake of confronting a man in his castle cost him?"

"It cost him a lot. Picture a head-on collision between a ten-speed bicycle and a front-end loader with a full load of gravel. Who do you think would win?"

"The heavy machinery, construction vehicle wins hands down. As my granddad used to say, only fools take risks without assessing them first. In this case, your lover was a certified fool."

"You are exactly right. My boy showed poor judgment. I realized right then that he was a fool. Despite his washboard abdomen, he was puny. On the other hand, my dad, whom my mom called a huge, strong beast, stood six foot two and weighed a solid 220 pounds of pure, nonsteroidal muscles, and despite a bad left knee, he was quick and had good aim.

"When the boy got in my father's face, Dad acted a gentleman at first and stepped back. I have no idea who advised my boy. It could not have been a boxing promoter hoping for an even match. The kid threw the first punch. He did not hit his target. Dad blocked the shot without breaking a sweat. Though he was not too much into scripture, my father firmly believed the biblical injunction that children should obey their elders at all times. He decided to teach the boy a lesson and to use all the hand-to-hand combat techniques the US military had taught him. He came down on my lover like a steamroller. He picked him up several times and tossed him across the room. After he was done, Dad kicked my lover's clothing and the case of unopened beer sitting on a stool toward the boy. Then he went into the entertainment room, disconnected the amp, and returned to the banquet hall as if nothing had happened.

"Just as Dad pulled out of our driveway, I saw a squad car approaching. I had no idea if my lover had used our home phone to summon the police or if they just happened to be passing by. I did not know what I was going to tell them, but I had a responsibility to act, because inside that house lay the only boy who did not fear of being shot if he got close enough to make a woman out of me. He was the only boy bold enough to do what I had always wanted done to me, and he could die for his gallantry.

Gripped by hysteria and with my hair disheveled, I flagged down the police and pointed them to our front door.

Guns drawn, the officers cautiously entered our house. They found a heavily tattooed young man without pants writhing on the floor, flanked by two pit bulls. The boy was in bad shape. Therefore, the police skipped informing him of his right to remain silent. Based on their training, the officers assumed that the young man had broken into the house and that the pit bulls had cornered him and attacked. They did not ask me any questions. They just got on their radio. An emergency vehicle soon arrived to transport my bad boy to the hospital."

"The police did not ask you to ride along or to make a statement?"

"No, there was no time for me to do either of those things."

"There was no time for you to do the right thing?"

"Well, instead of going to see if the boy would be all right, I had to return to the banquet hall to hunt down my friends and give them the good news that, like them, I was no longer a virgin, that I had finally gone all way with a boy. I was disappointed. They were not happy for me as I thought they would be."

"Why were your friends not happy that you had joined the ranks of the liberated?"

"They said there were no ranks to join. Instead of applauding me and my accomplishment, they rained on my parade by saying I had made a terrible mistake. They said that they all were still virgins, that when they bragged about going all the way with boys, they were just shooting the breeze. So you can see why going to check up on my bad boy would have been a good investment of my time."

CHAPTER 5

ON HER FIRST day back in middle school after the long summer break, Mary Yvette Louis felt light-headed and passed out in class. She was taken to the school nurse. The nurse could find nothing wrong with her but thought she was dehydrated. She gave Mary some glucose-enhanced water to drink and sent her back to the classroom, where she threw up. She was sleepy throughout the rest of the school day. Her teacher consulted with the nurse after another bout of vomiting. Mary was kept at the nurse's station until school adjourned. At home, she was fine. But the next day, she threw up on arriving at school and remained in the bathroom urinating and vomiting. The teacher went to check on her. Mary told her she had a bad cold. The teacher again sent her to the nurse, who determined that she had a virus. Her mom was called. She arrived and took Mary to a doctor.

At the doctor's, blood was drawn and tests were done. She was told to stay home from school until the nature of her ailment could be determined. Mary liked that. The results came back in a couple of days. The physician asked Mrs. Louis for permission to perform a sonogram on Mary. Her mom was alarmed that the doctor would make such a request, and she asked to speak to him. The doctor requested that she talk to him in person. She went, fuming. The doctor led her into his office and shut the door. He told her that a trace of human chorionic gonadotropin, or HGC, was detected in Mary's urine. Therefore, he needed to rule out pregnancy as the cause of her morning sickness. Mrs. Louis argued that her child simply had a cold, which kids often got when they were grouped together.

The doctor said he understood that, but since there had been instances in which teenagers gave birth without knowing or believing they were pregnant, he needed permission to probe further. He also wanted Mary's mom to ask her if she had done something she had no business doing. Mary furiously denied this.

The next time the doctor's office called, it was to tell her mom that in about six months, the cold that Mary had self-diagnosed would produce a baby girl.

After the news broke that Mary would soon become a mom, she started feeling terrible and hurt all over. Her heart hurt more because her friends, suspecting that her pregnancy, like the common cold, could be contagious, avoided her.

When the pregnancy was confirmed, Mr. Louis went down to the police station to file a rape charge against Francis Perry. But his daughter, the supposed victim, would not let the charge stick. She said Perry did not force himself on her as her father wrongly concluded.

"It was bad enough that I was involved in a serious offense, something Dad said was a sure path to poverty," Mary recalled. "However, with my refusal to back his claim that my pregnancy resulted from a criminal act by Perry, Dad was through with me. He told Mom he wanted me out of his house so that I would not infect my younger siblings with the virus of self-induced poverty. My mom said I had nowhere to go, but Dad said that was my problem, not his. He said the conditions for living under his roof were very clear, and I had violated them. He said that all non-taxpayers living under his roof, whether they were his children, his nephews, his nieces, or his cousins, had to abide by his rules without exception.

"Mom kept trying to soften him up, but Dad wouldn't budge. Mom tried again. Dad abruptly got up, grabbed Mom by the wrist, led her into the kitchen, and pointed to a copy of the Ten Commandments engraved on a golden plate mounted on the side of the kitchen cabinet. Mom had given him the plate when they married. He lifted up the frame, revealing a scroll, which he unfolded.

"'This is general order number one for this family. No drugs, hard or soft. No marijuana. No sex and definitely no pregnancy out of wedlock. Only married people are allowed to have sex under my roof. That is general order number one for the Louis family.' He said my pregnancy was proof that I had violated the general order. I had chosen to be a wayward child, set on sabotaging him. Therefore, he said, he did not care where my waywardness took me. He said it broke his heart to see me go, but I must go. Fortunately, he did not throw out my stuff. He expected me to move it out, so my stuff remained. Mom told me to keep a low profile so as not to antagonize him, to stay in my room, and to keep away from the common areas of the house until his anger abated. She wanted me to avoid him to reduce the risk that he would hurt me. Dad was that angry.

"One day, he came home from work and mom asked to have a meeting with him. He told her that if she intended to ask him to forgive and forget my immorality and to extend my stay in his house, the answer remained no. He would not forgive a child who disobeyed her parents.

"Dad had a routine that seemed like a ritual. Returning from work, he would get into the shower, visit with Mom, read the newspaper while eating dinner, talk with Mom again while she watched a comedy show on television, and then go to bed. One night as Dad sat down for supper, Mom ushered Frank Perry into the dining room and announced that he had something to tell Dad. My father put down his knife and fork and stood up.

"'Hey man, I just want to say that if the test shows that the thing inside your daughter is mine, I will stand by my baby momma, okay? I know you think I'm fixing to skip town on her, but I'm not. So be cool, okay?'

"Dad, moving a little bit faster than the speed of light, grabbed Perry by the neck and lifted him off of the floor. Thank goodness Perry came to talk to Dad in the dining area, with the wall-to-wall china cabinet behind the dining table. Dad would do anything, including turning the other cheek, to avoid damaging Mom's collection of fine china and figurines. Otherwise, he would have thrown Perry against the wall.

"Mom pleaded with Dad to put Perry down. Dad complied and set Perry down as gracefully as a category-five tornado making landing.

"'Now let's start all over, young man,' Dad said. 'Go out outside of my house and knock on the front door. After I have said, "Come in," you enter and say, "Good evening, sir."'

"Mom knew that as soon as Perry stepped out of the house, Dad would lock him out and would not let him back in. So she asked Perry to apologize to Dad.

"'You're violent. Why you tripping, man?' he asked Dad.

"'First of all, I am Mr. Louis to you. You got that? Second, this is my house and you are trespassing. Third, if I put bullet holes in you in my own house, which I intend to do shortly, under the law of this great state, it will be counted as self-defense. You dig? So leave my house now while you are still ahead of the game and before I exercise my inalienable right to protect my family and my castle against all invaders.'

"Mom pleaded with Dad to listen to what Perry had to say, but Dad told her, 'That punk has nothing to say to me. As far as I am concerned, he has already said all he had to say to me. Anything else he says will only increase the provocation and the chance that I will hurt him badly. I do not know what he is doing in my house, but if you invited him, be aware that he's antagonizing me and withdraw the invitation now before he gets hurt.'

"'Honey, remember that you and Mr. Mayfield have been saying that there are no foolish questions in life, so why not let the young man say what he came here to say? You can take it or leave it, but do not deny him the right to free speech. That is what you fought the fascists for.'

"'If he is not here to ask to marry your rebellious daughter, whom he has forced, without much effort, to become a high school dropout, then to me, all his questions qualify as foolish questions, and I do not want to hear any of them.'

"'Hey, man, how can you say that? How can you know what I got to say when I have not even said it yet? Are you claiming to be a mind reader, a psychic, or something?' Perry said.

"'It does not matter what I am. Dumbness may or may not be contagious, but a foolish man is incapable of producing wisdom. It is not in him. All nonsense may not sound the same, but it is nonsense nonetheless,' Dad said.

"'Honey, please let us be civil,' Mom pleaded.

"'Baby, listen to me. My parents did not go to college, and they did not know anyone who did. Your parents did not go to college, and they too did not know college-educated people except the ones they worked for. Our folks did not even finish high school, but they knew how to figure things out. They knew what worked and latched on to it, avoiding what did not work. They learned the formula for escaping poverty. That is the reason they made sure we graduated from high school. We are not rich, because I did not go to college and you did not go to college. Therefore, it behooves us not just to push our kids to be their best selves but to make sure they graduate from college. High school dropouts dress like this punk. See how they walk? See how they talk? They are not aspiring for success. We should not permit our kids to do worse than their parents did. A college education is the avenue to doing better than their parents. That is what our parents found out and codified. Pregnancy without marriage and while still in high school kills that ascendancy. It renders that formula null and void.'

"'Honey, you know as well as I do that college is not for everyone.'

"'How about leaning a trade?'

"'Trade schools are not for everyone, either.'

"'Oh baby, it is so comforting to me to know that there is no weapon against self-induced poverty!'

"'Do not talk like that, honey. People have dropped out of college and still made it. They are not in the majority, but there is a long list of them out there.'

"'Is that my first child's excuse for not finishing high school, and are you as her ambassador conveying that message to me?'

"'No, I did not say that.'

"'What are you saying then?'

"'I am saying that two wrongs do not make a right. I'm saying that in real life, mistakes will be made. Therefore, do not throw away the baby with the bathwater. Do not be that cruel.'

"'Okay, tell me how I ended up being the bad guy here?'

"'Honey, I did not say you did anything wrong.'

"'Well, I was just about to say that though the story may not have received wide publicity, not only have I been a very good father, providing for my children economically and morally, but I have also been a very good husband to their mother, my wife. By that I mean I have never run around on my wife. Not a lot of men can make that claim. That is a fact. So no child of mine can credibly say she is wayward as a reaction to her old man's nefarious activities. I have not abused liquor, sneaked around behind her mom's back, or made babies out of wedlock.'

"'Honey, sometimes things happen despite our best efforts to prevent them. Kids are unpredictable like that. Parents can do only so much and should not commit suicide when their kids do the unthinkable.'

"'Did Dr. Albert Einstein say that?'

"'No.'

"'So you just made that up to excuse bad behavior? I like that in a mother.'

"'No, not exactly!'

"'Your argument is invalid. Here is what is valid. If you do the same thing all the time, you will get the same result all the time. As I testified, I have stayed around and raised this family with love and compassion. Mr. Mayfield has done the same. How come all his children are heading for college while my daughter is heading for a maternity hospital? Yes, I have failed in my responsibility as a dad! My main investment has not yielded any dividend. Why then I should hold myself up as a good, responsible father when, under my roof, a child of mine would willingly enter what she knew was going to be a temporary liaison with a drug abuser that has the potential of producing a bastard?'

"'As I said, this situation is not a reflection on you, honey.'

"'Well, thank you for that vote of confidence and for the truckload of comfort and consolation it has brought me. But the fact remains that although we cannot tell how things will turn out based on how and when they started, we do know that irresponsible pregnancy damages not just the unprepared-for baby but the teen mother as well. And that is under a normal circumstance. What we have here in my house is not a normal circumstance. For all we know, the police and the folks at Crime Detectors could very well be on this punk's trail. Your daughter brought to my house a lazy, filthy drug abuser, a first-class knucklehead, and a small-time thief. Together, they irresponsibly assembled the building blocks for a new life that they are incapable of providing for. And you expect me to roll out the red carpet because it is no big deal that young girls are not abstaining anymore? We also grew up in an era when young people did whatever felt good whenever it felt good to do it, but not every young person jumped on that fast-moving bandwagon. There are certain boundaries you cross at your eternal peril. Do you know how many other bastards this punk has produced?'

"'Hey, man, stop hating. Stop judging me by your standard. Tell me this: Who died and made you king?'

"'No one made me a ruler, certainly not over you. You are right about that. But you are standing in the house of a man who happens to know that success has a formula. Therefore, I insist that my kids avoid the likes of you, perpetual failures and take advantage of the opportunities this great nation offers even to those who were not born in this land, even to those who speak with an accent but are willing to work hard. I want my kids to see education as their ticket out of poverty.'

"'You are not holy yourself. You are not a righteous man by any means. You eat flesh. I do not. Therefore, do not sit in judgment.'

"'Is that because you, like other drug abusers, are always broke and cannot afford to buy meat, or is it because you're too lazy—in addition to lacking the skill—to go out to the forest to hunt game?'

"'No, I do not eat meat as a matter of religion. Unlike you, who take pride in flipping hamburger patties and finding joy in wolfing down assorted meats, I am a vegetarian. That should count for something.'

"'Of course it does. Okay, next question: what type of job do you have and how long have you been doing it?'

"'I do not have a job.'

"'It figures. Does that surprise anyone?'

"'What do you mean?'

"'As if your extensive rap sheet were not enough of an impediment to landing a job, appearing as trashy and as threatening as you do, no employer in his right mind would offer you a position—even in an oil field, where ex-convicts are given second chances because of the chain-gang nature of the work. Appearance matters. When was the last time you combed, clipped, or washed your hair?'

"'For your information, combs and scissors are not permitted on my head. I am a righteous man, a Nazarite. Nazarites do not cut or comb their hair. In addition, we have great understanding because unlike you, we are slow to wrath.'

"'Yes, prophet, as part of worship, you are allowed to abuse alcohol, smoke marijuana, and lead astray underage girls, but you do not worry about your appearance. What a religion! No wonder some young and misguided girls find your unkempt look cool.'

"'Hey man, you're still judging my worth based on my appearance and on other people's standards of excellence. What part of righteousness do you not understand? You do not know about my vision, do you?'

"'I did not know that your ilk had a vision other than going to Africa and sitting under some mango trees and smoking ganja all day long.'

"'You judge people and hate your fellow man. You have a closed mind and cannot see the vision of peace that we see.'

"'If the vision in your head does not include a job, or if you are into self-indulgent, negative behavior, that vision becomes a waste of time and a hallucination.'

"'I am not hallucinating.'

"'You and your type do illegal and immoral things under the guise of religion. You have no job but claim to have money. You have been smoking something that is not good for you. It causes you to see things that are not there. You call it a vision. The rest of the world knows it as a hallucination.'

"'And you are full of wrath because you lack understanding. Looks like you were raised without love, in a household filled with lots of abuses'

"What did you just call my mother? Dad asked.

"'You heard me loud and clear,' Perry replied.

"'Young man, you have overstayed your welcome. This is my house. I know for a fact that it has at least four exits. Take one of them before you get hurt. You are persona non grata here. Leave my house right now.'

"'Oh yeah? Make me.'

"Dad and Perry began to circle each other. Mom picked up the telephone from the kitchen counter and dialed.

"In five minutes or less, a squad car pulled up in front of our home. An officer walked up the driveway and knocked on the door. Mom opened the door and let the officer in. The officer did not draw her weapon but placed a hand on the butt of the service revolver. She asked Mom what was the matter.

"Mom told the officer that Perry had trespassed at our home and that Dad had asked nicely that Perry leave for his own safety. Perry quickly accused Dad of assault and showed the officer what he said were wounds on his body. The officer radioed her partner to come in. The other officer waited until backup arrived before entering the house. The officers put on latex gloves and examined Perry. The marks did not look like they had just been inflicted. The officers wanted to know who caused the marks and when. Perry hesitated. It appeared that he was trying to make up a story. The female officer took a pair of handcuffs from her belt and asked Perry to tell them what was really going on, since what he called fresh wounds were actually scars.

"Mom explained the situation to the officers. She told them that Dad had expected his first daughter to be a role model for the rest of his children. Since I had shown signs of being exceptionally smart at a very young age, I was expected not only to be a success academically but to remain a virgin until after college. Mom said I seemed to have been following my father's script until Perry came along. She said he tricked me into fooling around with him, and I not only lost my virginity but became pregnant, causing me to drop out of high school and dashing my father's hope that I would be the first in his family to graduate from college. Mom begged the officers to intercede. The officers asked Dad for his side of the story. He said he wanted Perry to restore my virginity, which he had stolen from me. They asked him for a reasonable alternative, since even in the high-tech era his first choice was unachievable. Dad said that since Perry was the type of knucklehead who made babies indiscriminately without a thought about how to provide for them, a restraining order should be issued and strictly enforced to keep Perry from contacting me or any member of the Louis clan.

"The officers asked to see Perry's identification, anything with his picture on it. He had none. They asked where he worked and what type of work he did. He said he did not have a job.

"'It figures," Dad said.

"Then Perry revised his response. He said he was a self-employed businessman.

"'And what of type business are you involved in, Mr. Perry?' one officer asked.

"'Excuse me, officers,' Dad said. "Did you not hear the first answer that punk gave you?'

"'Yes, we did, sir,' one officer said.

"'It doesn't seem like you did,' Dad replied.

"'What did we miss, Mr. Louis?' the officer asked.

"'Not only doesn't he have a job," Dad said, 'but he is proud of that. He has no intention of looking for or getting a job anytime soon because that would leave him less time to foist evil on little girls when they are expected to be in school and their parents are at work. He is an incorrigible child predator. That's what he's telling you'

"'I am sorry, Mr. Louis, but we did not hear him say that,' one officer said.

"'See? That's him. He's good at putting words in my mouth,' Perry interjected.

"'Go ahead, Mr. Louis,' the officer said. 'You said we missed something.'

"'You have not had the chance to research him as I have,' Dad said. 'This hard-drug abuser has fooled not just others but him-self into believing he is a dealer and therefore will eventually hit it big.'

"'Tell us more, Mr. Louis,' the officer said.

"'I do not know how long you have been with the department, but you should be familiar with this rotten egg,' Dad said. 'He has a rap sheet at least a mile long. When y'all have time, look at the juvenile records and you will find out that this punk lives for trouble. He started his criminal career long ago. He will never make something out of himself, because he is not trying. When he was twelve, he and his friends took an expensive car for a joy ride. Police noticed that the driver's head was barely visible above the steering wheel. They got behind the car and turned on their cruiser's red-and-blue lights. The car took off and the police gave chase.

"When the car hit a guardrail and stopped at the Quitman exit on the Loop East, the pint-size driver was found passed out. He was taken to the hospital. Tests showed that to hide the evidence, he had ingested a large amount of illegal drugs. The plastic bags that had held the drugs littered the floor of the automobile. His mom was brought in for questioning to determine if she was dealing drugs. She was not but admitted that one day while doing laundry, she found a hundred-dollar bill in Perry's pocket. She said she kept the money and her son did not miss it. She said that when she asked him where the money came from, he would not tell her. Because of his age, he did not do time for that crime, and he took that to mean he had a license to commit more crimes.

"'At thirteen, he punched the lights out of his teacher, and after he threatened another teacher with a box cutter, he was sent to an alternative school. The next year, he attacked his grandmother for not letting him pawn her VCR.'

"'Mr. Louis, is this the same kid who skipped school to go around damaging folks' property and who was finally arrested in Roadrunner Village for breaking into people's cars?' the female officer asked.

"'He's the same one,' Dad said.

"'In that case,' she said, 'I remember him very well. He did no time for those infractions. At a juvenile detention hearing, he convinced us that he was traumatized and acting out because his African father left him and his mother to bring another woman back from Africa. After he told that story about being deprived of love and fatherly direction, there wasn't a dry eye in court. Everyone, including prosecutors, was sympathetic. They pleaded for the kid to be released to the custody of his mom, and he was. We had eggs on our faces shortly after that. His grandmother called us to have him removed from her house.'

"'As the folksy news commentator used to say on the radio, "Now here is the rest of the story,"' Dad said. 'The man he blamed for sparking his evildoing was not his biological father. Records show the man had a master's in mental health and was a licensed counselor. Perry's mom worked at a fast-food restaurant that the man managed. Well, one thing led to another and the man ended up marrying his employee. Records show he fathered only one kid, a little girl, with this woman, but he bought a big house to accommodate all of her kids. At the urging of his fellow Africans, the man quickly moved out of his own house after Perry pistol-whipped him.'

"'What happened, Mr. Louis?' the female officer asked.

"'The man did not want to lose his professional licenses,' Dad said, 'and so he asked his wife why she had permitted Perry to host a party where underage drinking had taken place. Perry's mom did not think it was a big deal for her kid and his friends to cut loose a little. After that, Perry went a step further. He moved an underage girl with a newborn baby into the house without bothering to ask permission. The man told his wife that harboring a minor was a major infraction of the law and that the girl and her baby should return to her parents. He said no minor was allowed to move into the house unless the move was cleared with him first. The next day, the man came home from work to find the master bedroom ransacked. He asked Perry what he knew about the vandalism. Perry stood toe to toe with the man and said, "I should have blown out your brains when I had the chance, but I did not want to splatter your weak blood on my beautiful momma asleep beside you. You won't be so lucky next time. That's a promise.'"

"'I remember this story,' the male officer said.

"'It is a sad, but a true story. I am not fibbing,' Dad said. 'After the man moved out, Perry's mom struggled. The bank holding the mortgage refused to refinance the house because it was not on her name. They told her she could continue to live in the house, so long as she was sending in the rents. The house had a sun roof and a cathedral ceiling, so the heating bill was huge. And with so many mouths to feed, she was not only behind on the mortgage and the property tax bills but on the light and the water bills as well. The bank foreclosed on the house. That was when grand mom opened her doors and gave them a place to stay.

"'It did not take this criminal long to prove to his grand mom that she had made a huge mistake by inviting him to come in from the cold. And that is the kind of character whom my daughter has brought home and whom my wife has allowed to darken the doorway of my house—a character who by choice is nothing now and who by choice will never amount to anything. And now my daughter is dropping out of high school for the dubious honor of having him call her "my baby momma."'"

"'Officers, you have a duty to arrest this man,' Perry said. 'He has just admitted to some serious criminal activities. This is not some backwater nation. The records of minors interacting with the law are sacred documents in this country. How did this man get access to those?'

"The officers asked Perry what he knew about my pregnancy and what was he going to do about it. I jumped in and said Perry and I were going to get married. I did not clear that wish with him first.

"'Hey, watch it, girl,' Perry said. 'That may be what you want for you and your baby, but that is not what I want for me. So do not put words in my mouth, okay? You are just like your old man. You all like putting words in my mouth like I'm a baby. For one thing, I do not want be a part of your family. There's just no way!'

"Perry told the officers that he was too young to get married but that if a DNA test showed that the baby was his, which he doubted, he would see what he could do to help out his baby's momma."

"'Did you hear that?" Dad said. "I cannot stand that nonchalant attitude. He is not too young to make a baby here, a baby there, and babies all over the place, but all of a sudden, he's too young to take responsibility for his evil actions. That is the type of vomit that convinces me I would be doing the world a big favor if I took this stinking drug user out of circulation or least beat his behind.' Dad took a few steps toward Perry, who threw an uppercut that was about a foot short of its target. Dad leaned forward and slapped it down hard with his palm. Perry flinched and cursed.

"'Tell us the reason you said what you just said, Mr. Perry,' the female officer said.

"'Well, the old man is making it sound like all this is my fault.'

"'Is it not?' the officer asked.

"'No, it is not,' Perry said. 'How does he know that I am her only customer?'

"'That is an interesting question and noun selection,' the male officer said. 'Do you know of other customers? Why did you decide to be with a girl who was that popular? Are you willing to name names to reduce your responsibility?'

"'Not exactly,' Perry said, 'but you can ask her. If she is as well-raised as her old man says, telling the truth should come naturally for her, right? She knows where she has been and the guys she has been with. I have been with her only half of one time, and that was at her insistence. Doing the little we did has never been known to create the problem she now has. A DNA test will show the truth. And do not let her demeanor fool y'all. She is aggressive. I did not start this. Maybe she ran after other guys like she did me. She is not my type. Mary initiated this. She knows the truth. She asked me to take her away from the boring and nerdy boys her old man was forcing her to go with. I did her a favor and went along with her. What wrong did I do? Why should my act of kindness be held against me? If anything, I should be compensated for providing urgent help to a girl to escape an abusive dad.'

"'Okay, but now your help has become unhelpful,' the male officer said. 'It has backfired, as you know too well. An unplanned-for pregnancy has resulted. What are you going to do about it? What are you going to do to remedy the situation?'

"'Don't look at me. I can do nothing,' Perry said.

"'You know that because you went along with her plans, which you said were imposed on you, her father's house is no longer available to her?' the officer said.

"'Yeah, you feel me? He is always judging people. He's so full of himself. What kind of dad is that? He's not fit to be a dad. The man needs to chill out. He acts like he's above the law or something.'

"'Do not worry about what he is doing,' the officer said. 'What are you going to do about your woman and your baby?'

"'Hey, that man violated my rights,' Perry said. 'Y'all need to take him downtown. You are the law. Do something about him. Slap cuffs on him. Otherwise, I am going to make a citizen's arrest of him right now.'

"'You are going to make a citizen's arrest?' the female officer asked Perry.

"'You're damned straight,' Perry replied.

"'And what are the grounds for a citizen's arrest?' she asked.

"'It's okay for him to look down on me,' Perry said. 'He looks down on me because my mother is a single mom. That is the reason he is asking for a restraining order on me. But he can't go around looking down on the police. That's the law.'

"'Looking down on people is un-Christian, but it is completely legal,' the female officer said. 'If we took people to jail for that, not only would we run out of jail space, but we would be violating those people's rights.'

"'Then arrest him for false impersonation,' Perry said.

"'False impersonation? What do you mean?' the officer asked.

"'The man admitted that he did not go to college, but he is so full of adulation for college folks as if college has given them the ability to walk on water,' Perry said. 'But I know real college people. They wear dreadlocks. They smoke weed and cover themselves with body art, which this old guy still calls tattoos. But I will have him know that tattoos are no longer confined to prisons. They have been rebranded and have gone mainstream. Even bankers are sporting them. So he should stop impersonating college folks and looking down on my mom because I wear body art.'

"'Only a certified crackhead could talk such nonsense,' Dad said. 'How can I hate his mom? How could any sane person hold her responsible for the actions of her irresponsible, drug-abusing son? For all I know, the woman may find herself in the same boat that I am in. My child does not listen to me. I can't assume that this poor woman's poor excuse for a son listens to her either.'

"'You look down on my mom because she has no husband,' Perry said.

"'You saw to that, remember? Why would I blame her for being a single mom?' Dad said.

"'Mr. Perry, try not to worry about the wrong thing, okay?' the female officer said. 'It may distract us, but it is not going to solve the problem that you have helped to create. You made an adult decision, and now that you are faced with an adult consequence, be an adult. It's time to grow up. Come up with a solution. That's what adults do. Dragging your mom into the mess is easy to do, but it won't solve the problem. The problem is real.'

"'Like I said, marriage is out,' Perry replied. 'It does not matter what this man thinks of me and my mom. I do not want to make promises I cannot keep just so I can prove him wrong. Also, I cannot take this girl home with me. We live in the hood. She is better off staying with her folks. My mom lives in a tiny apartment and she hates it.'

"'Mr. Perry, you are obviously a very intelligent young man, so why didn't you think through all these variables earlier?' the officer asked.

"'I am a victim of the war in this family,' Perry said. 'These people can't get along, but since they have standing in this community, they want to make it seem like outsiders are to blame.'

"'Come on, man!' the male officer said.

"'Like I told you, this was not my call,' Perry said. 'She is not my type. I was merely doing her a favor. She wanted to be liberated from a tyrant dad so she could be free like her friends.'

"'Her making a baby while a child herself is not exactly freedom,' the male officer said. 'Would you agree?'

"'I strongly disagree. I helped only on the liberation front,' Perry said.

"'Well, seeing that in wars, neither liberators nor peacekeepers are guaranteed victories without risks, don't you think you bear some responsibility for your woman's impending motherhood?' the male officer asked.

"'No, I do not,' Perry said. 'Number one, she is not my woman. Number two, if that man kicks her out of this old, beat-up excuse for a house, which he is mistaking for a mansion just because it is not located in the hood, she can do like my mom did after my dad abandoned her for a woman from Africa. She can always stay at the Promised Comforter House, the Teenage Mothers' Refuge, or the Highway of Hope Housing Estate.'

"'Is that your standard?' Dad asked. 'Since your mother sought refuge in shelters, you believe it is your responsibility to make sure every young girl ends up there?'

"Before Perry could answer, Dad rushed him again and grabbed him by the shirt collar. The officers intervened.

"'Gentlemen, as they say in boxing, return to your corners, please,' the male officer said. 'I want everyone to be as non-confrontational as possible. That way we won't need to transport anyone downtown for fingerprinting, a green jumpsuit, a mug-shot, and all the other good stuff. Please talk to each other with civility.'

"'We need action, officers,' Dad said. 'The public isn't well served by having you spend your shift in this house being played by a professional con artist. I do not mean to be disrespectful, but have we not talked too much without saying anything?'

"'It may very well appear so. But you must continue to talk to each other. Dialogue can only help. There is a problem that needs to be solved, and you have that common interest. Therefore, please choose your words carefully and get your points across without being belligerent and ugly. Though many conflicts are taking place in the Third World right now, those skirmishes have not goaded the First World into starting a Third World War. That is a good thing, a function of patience and of dialogue at the United Nations. If the earth, which is divided by several oceans, twenty-four time zones, a million languages, and power-hungry politicians, has prevented a third big war for this long, you two people should be able to tolerate each other. Is that a deal?'

"'No deal. I'd rather go to jail than sit here and allow a common criminal to insult and mock me in my own house,' Dad said.

"'Mr. Louis …" the male officer cautioned.

"'Officers, see that space on the wall?'

"'Yes,' the male officer said. 'What about it?'

"'My daughter's diploma was supposed to go on that spot,' Dad said. 'Since the day my wife and I brought her home from the hospital, that space has been reserved for the embossed piece of paper high schools issue to kids when they pay attention, endure, and complete the second tier of their formal education. I also had the dream of being that happy papa we see walking his little girl down the aisle to be united in holy matrimony with a decent man whom that daddy would not be ashamed to call a son-in-law. I had drummed into her head that college, not high school, is the ideal place to look for a husband, because almost everyone there is determined to belong to the middle class. That admonition fell on deaf ears.

"'Now, to add insult to injury, the knucklehead who violated her and kept her from reaching her educational potential can't even make a decent woman out of her in front of a Justice of the Peace, much less offer the societal wedding I have been dreaming of. That means this reserved space won't see my daughter's high school diploma or her marriage license signed by a clergyman with a doctoral degree. So why am I required to reconcile with the drug dealer who turned my dreams into nightmares? Where is the justice in that?'

"'Mr. Louis, your daughter made a mistake,' the male officer said. 'It is a given that if we live long, at some point in life, we will run into disappointments, many of them. You, sir, are a leader in this community, and therefore you have seen this same disappointment befall other people who did not ask for it. Because of your prominent position, I bet you may have provided a shoulder for others to cry on. Now that you have experienced your own heartbreak, are you going to put yourself beyond consolation? If so, why? Surely you know your daughter can always go back to school after she has had her baby. This is where the community and its resources come in, to salvage the unsalvageable.'

"'Putting the cart before the horse is popular in some circles, but it is a losing proposition,' Dad said. 'This arrangement has never worked, and I am sure it won't work for me. Who will take care of my daughter's child while she halfheartedly tries to reconstruct her messed-up life? Certainly, it won't be me. I was not raised by my grandparents. Since I live by example, I do not plan on raising my grandchildren. They can visit if their parents have lived by my general order, but they can't stay. When the parents leave, the grandkids leave too.'

"'You are right, Mr. Louis,' the male officer replied. 'Your kid has messed up big time, but she is neither the first nor will she be the last underage girl to fall into the pit that her hormone-propelled foolishness dug for her. However, again, all is not lost. As you very well know, the local government has resources to help her out. She can rejoin the race to the top. All it takes is the determination to do so and your support.'

"'First of all, my kid should learn from me,' Dad said. 'I pride myself on never going on the public dole. I worked even in poor health. Second, with a knucklehead like that drug abuser by her side, she'll be likely to do more of the same. They will continue making bastards indiscriminately. That mission will consume her whole life, and she intends on stressing me to an early death with it. I respectfully decline to go along with that plan.

"'Yes, she may rejoin the quest for a better life, but she will never catch up. There is a time and a place for everything, and it is much easier to climb the ladder of success when you are not lugging a twenty-five-pound weight."

"'Don't worry, Daddy. I will get a GED," I said.

"'Get a GED?' Dad asked.

"'Yes, Daddy. I know I can get a job with a GED,' I told him. 'I know some kids with GEDs who got jobs. I will make sure Frankie gets a job too.'

"'You mean two of you will get jobs with just one GED?' Dad asked.

"'No, Daddy. Frankie will get his own GED,' I said.

"'How will he do that, considering he cannot read? I don't think they have invented a verbal GED yet,' Dad said,

"'Daddy, are you saying Frankie cannot read?' I asked.

"'No, I'm saying he can neither read nor write,' Dad replied. 'He did not stay in school long enough to learn how to color within the lines. If he cannot spell his own name, tell me how he can read. Did he tell you differently?'

"'He never discussed school with me,' I replied.

"'Why doesn't that surprise me?' Dad shot back.

"'Honey,' Mom said, 'Frank can read. How could he have passed his written driving test if he could not read?'

"'The short answer,' Dad said, 'is that like most criminals, he has been operating motor vehicles unlawfully, without a valid driver's license.'

"'Tell him you have a driver's license, Frankie baby,' Mom said.

"'Baby, if he says he has one, he is lying, which would not be out of character for him. He has a thing against licenses,' Dad said.

"'Daddy, his car has license plates on it,' I said.

"'My former daughter,' Dad said, 'I know that our schools no longer teach English literature. Therefore, you may not be familiar with the name William Shakespeare, but he foresaw the situation that you have put yourself in and issued a warning: 'If one should be a prey, how much the better to fall before the lion than the wolf.'

"'I do not know the fault lines social engineers of the future will find in my parental style, but as much as I hate the undeserved shame that you have heaped on me and my family, it will soon dawn on you that you have hurt yourself more than you have hurt me with your wildness. You have set yourself up to struggle all your life in the valley of humiliation. Just wait until you find out how many other babies that punk has made with other daddy-disobeying and thug-loving little girls just like you. You will never have a future with this drug addict. And that is not only because his plans do not include you, but more important, because he has no future. One of these days, he will be on the evening news, dead.'

"'Jack!'" Mom said sternly.

"'Listen to me, baby,' Dad said. 'That is the bitter truth, and you can take it to the bank. Your daughter has disobeyed and hurt me with your consent, but she will spend the rest of her life paying for what she has done.'

"'God forbid,' Mom said.

"'It is a little bit late for that,' Dad replied. "The situation is a lot like gravity: there's no reverse gear in it."

"'Why?' Mom asked.

"'It may not apply in movies, but the law of distributive justice applies to real life in real time,' Dad said. 'As King Solomon said, unrighteousness brings death.'

"'King Solomon did not say that, honey,' Mom replied. 'He had everything going for him, including a thousand women, every one of them fighting for his attention. He was too positive a guy to make a negative statement like that.'

"'You are right,' Dad said. 'He actually said that righteousness brings life. I gave you the flip side of that statement.'

"'Honey, are you wishing evil on your own child?' Mom asked.

"'No, baby. My child has already chosen evil,' Dad replied. 'I am merely restating the provisions of the Law of Distributive Justice as it applies to those of us lucky enough to live on earth. They may have it differently on other planets, but on earth, people usually reap what they sow, even when they sow in secret. Therefore, parents should not post bail bonds or hire fiery lawyers so their kids can sidestep the consequences of their excesses. Every action comes with a consequence, period. As hard as we try, we cannot separate an action from an equal and opposite reaction. That provision is carved in granite, and nothing can change it.'

"'Honey, you may not have noticed it, but kids these days do not know that, neither do they care,' Mom said.

"'Though ignorance of the law has never been accepted as a good defense for breaking it, you are right,' Dad said. 'The Law of Distributive Justice is indeed an archaic law. Some people are not aware of its existence at all, and others, surrounded by a popular culture that claims it is okay to say whatever comes to mind and to do whatever feels good, deny that such a law is on the books. But in its natural form, that Mosaic Law was literally carved in stone and does not change with the cultural winds. This law guarantees that those who live right will enjoy the good life. On the other hand, those who flout moral boundaries to pursue the good life and who disregard parental admonitions will end up living short, tortured lives.'

"'Mr. Louis, your wife is right,' the female officer said. 'Even if society had laws governing every facet of life with lockups on every block, we still would have people who could not or would not conform to our highest ideals. Therefore, we must temper justice with mercy. The community—churches, social organizations, and law enforcement—must do more than hold the feet of our young to the fire. In addition to holding the safety nets, we must sometimes be the safety nets ourselves, particularly at the critical moments when the little darlings we are trying to save from themselves produce our biggest headaches and disappointments.'

"'Officers, is it asking too much to expect the fruit not to fall far from the tree?' Dad wondered. 'When a kid like mine, who is not yet qualified to vote, chooses fornication over her education, she might as well be jumping from the Texas Tower of Commerce Building. Since no safety net has yet been designed to prevent such self-destruction, no dad should be expected to put his life on hold for eighteen more years to correct the deliberate sins of his child. That would be too much punishment for an innocent man like me. Let us follow the Law of Moses on this. Do not punish a dad for the waywardness of his child. Let a child who chose to put herself between a rock and a hard place be held responsible for her sins. She had made her bed. Now let her lie in it.'

"'Your analogy is right on the money, Mr. Louis,' the female officer replied. 'But the boundary-defying excesses and the reckless abandon of our kids do not absolve us parents from being the guidance counselors and protectors we were designed to be. Sometimes we forget our primary roles in the lives of these experimenters called children. Forgive the expression, but we need to man up. All of the formal and informal training we have ever received—whether from juvenile detention centers, Sunday schools, churches, schools, or Boy Scouting—was preparing us for the unscripted situations that life presents. Therefore, we must not give up when all our ducks, for one reason or another, are not in a row.'

"'Officers, here's an update,' Dad said. 'The doors to my house will always be open to any child of mine, or any other child for that matter, who stumbles and falls in the process of escaping poverty. Any child who recognizes as I do, and as my parents did, that it's not good to be poor and is trying to make something of him-self or her-self, instead of being the cause of his or her poverty, is welcome in my house anytime. On the other hand, my children who aim not just to live in poverty but to drag me into it, and to kill me with stress by recklessly producing kids for me to raise, will find that the doors to my castle are not just closed but sealed shut. If that makes me a bad dad, so be it. This is not a new provision. In my house obedience is absolute. If you listen to me, you live under my roof. If you prefer to listen to your friends and to live as you please, I am disappointed but not mad at you. However, you must leave and live with them. There is no middle ground.'

"'Mr. Louis, there seems to be a power struggle going on here,' the female officer replied. 'Though we do not want to take sides, we wish you could see your wife's perspective on this matter. It buttresses the point that although our kids will not always listen to us, our roles as their guidance counselors and protectors remain undiminished. We are begging you not to kick your daughter out of your house. She has no job and no marketable skills. Where would she go? They are too many wolves out there in the world waiting to devour misguided kids like her. Do not deny your child the protection that only you, her father, can provide.'

"'Officers, it seems to me that you and I are not communicating,' Dad said. 'You said she's a misguided kid. That came across as accusatory to me. I did not misguide her. She misguided herself. If you cannot make that distinction, maybe you should leave before I raise my voice at you. I used to be in uniform for Uncle Sam. I hold uniforms in high esteem. As a result, I do not want to disrespect your uniforms and what they represent by throwing you out of my house.'

"'That's okay, Mr. Louis. We are humans just like you are,' the female officer said.

"'The bottom line is that I won't let that woman stay in my house, period,' Dad said. 'The first reason is that it is not economical: you do not invite a camel to share an eight-by-eight tent with your family. If you bring the animal into that enclosure, you are sure to find yourself without shelter, because a camel is not a puppy and should not be expected to act like one. By the same token, if I allowed that pregnant woman to stay here, I would be doing harm to my other kids. They would gladly follow the principle of 'monkey see, monkey do.' They would see nothing wrong with dropping out of middle school to have babies for common thieves and drug abusers. Yes, I am not a very good dad, but I have a responsibility to leave the world a better place than that. So I am going to make sure that the kids who are abiding by my rules are not exposed to the contaminants of the one who chooses to run the streets, the one who does not want to hear how consequences are related to actions. The second reason is self-preservation.'

"'What do you mean?' the female officer asked.

"'This car thief, the permanently jobless punk and wannabe drug dealer she has brought into my house, is likely to shoot me one of these days. My former child must have told him that I have money. As an addict, he will always need his fix. And given that job prospects for him in this economy are worse than bleak and that he is too lazy a criminal to rob a bank, he would have to steal my electronics and my money to feed his drug habit. The third reason is that I should not be allowed to share space with a wayward child. I might hurt her and end up in prison and deny my kids, particularly the fifth-grader, a chance at normal childhood.'

"'You know that much, so do the right thing,' the female officer said. 'Control your anger and restrain yourself, Mr. Louis. Our kids put us through a lot.'

"'Tell me about it!' Dad said.

"'But despite the pains we suffer at their hands, we cannot be so inconsolable, so emotionally distraught, that we feel the answer to the hurt lies in chucking our kids out on the street,' the female officer said.

"'Miss, did your child ever slap you across your face?' Dad asked. 'Have you been in this situation?'

"'No, I have not, Mr. Louis,' she said.

"'Then there is just no way you can know what it feels like to have your child kick you to the ground and drag you face-down through the mud,' Dad said.

"'No, I have not had that experience,' the officer said.

"'My grand-mother was a very active woman before suffering an aneurysm,' Dad said. 'When acquaintances and friends saw her struggling to do things able-bodied people do without much thought, they used to sympathize with her by saying they knew what she was going through. She used to respond that only people who had strokes would know the pain they caused. My grandma told people that if she had enemies, she would not wish the pain of a stroke on the worst of them. In order words, unless you have walked a mile in my shoes, you cannot feel my pain, officers. Only he who feels it knows it. So when you advise me to straighten up and walk right after my child has bloodied me, poised to drag my family back into poverty, you are asking me to do something that is not just hard but impossible.'

"'Of course it is hard, and not everyone can do it, but we trust that you can,' the male officer said. 'It is like playing football at a professional level. It is not easy, but the game's elite, even when playing hurt, make it look easy. You are an outstanding member of this community, an elite player. Play at the top of your game. Show others how it is done. This is when leadership by example is called for.'

"'Thanks for the flattery,' Dad said, 'but as far as that woman is concerned, we are through. I have swept her into the trash can. She is no longer my child.'

"'God forbid. Do not say that,' the officer replied. 'You are a good man, Mr. Louis. Expand your goodness by being forgiving. Forgiveness is the hallmark of deeply good people, not of the superficial ones.'

"'I forgive plenty, Dad said. 'Although I am not aiming to have my name enshrined in the hall of fame dedicated to the most forgiving people, I do forgive plenty.'

"'But your forgiveness does not extend to family?' the male officer asked.

"'I forgive family members' mistakes but not their acts of sabotage,' Dad said.

"'Let me tell you this, Mr. Louis,' the female officer said. 'In the years my partner and I have been with the department, we have never before been called to this home in response to a domestic situation. In most cases, the upheavals are usually caused by the heads of families, the men. But in your own case, we have testimony from a very reliable source, your wife, that you are an outstanding man, a man who lives for his family.'

"'I do not know about that,' Dad said. 'My wife used to have my back, but since her daughter made a laughingstock of me by bloodying me up and giving me this black eye, my wife has been pitching opposite me. In fact, the way it is going now, this marriage is worse than being on life support. Therefore, I need to be very careful around her, because as your Miranda warning states, anything I say can and will be used against me.'

"'According to the rule of evidence, we do not foresee divorce in your future,' the female officer said. 'Mrs. Louis says you are her rock. A woman does not say that about her man one day and hire a divorce lawyer the next. A rock, as we know from the Good Book, is a place of security, a refuge and a shelter from what is not wholesome. And your wife says you are that rock.'

"'Then I take it you do not know much about humans, particularly women and their tendency to change with the season,' Dad replied.

"'Mr. Louis, I am a woman inside and outside,' the officer said. 'I have been married to the same man for all of my adult life, but I have not called him my rock. I am not alone. Most women won't say that. I won't call my husband my rock, because I do not know where he is or what he is doing while I'm out keeping the peace in our community. Your wife has no such qualms about the man who put that ring on her finger many years ago. That to me is worth a lot.

"'All your wife is asking is that you be there for your daughter as well, even with her foibles, especially now when she needs you most. When your wife says that you are a good man, we do not fact-check it. We have no doubt that you are.'

"'No, officers, do not pull my leg like that. Had I been that good a dad and husband, if I were the roaring success you are implying, it would undoubtedly have rubbed off on all my kids. They would have emulated me, their live-in role model. That's how things work. Success breeds success.'

"'It's not an exact science. The reality is that for the most part, peer pressure and the neighborhood influence kids more than parents do,' the female officer said.

"'That is not true either,' Dad said. 'Her customer made one true statement tonight. He said she is not a product of the so-called hood. A child who emulates her dad will turn out different no matter how bad the neighborhood in which she grows up. As it stands now, I merely did my duty and nothing else, and that is the reason this woman behaved as if I were an absentee dad.'

"'Mr. Louis, do not sell your-self short,' the female officer said. 'Mrs. Louis considers herself blessed. She says that in the years since you made her your bride, her car has never broken down. You sacrificed for this family. Are you saying she is lying when she says you treat her like a queen and your children like royals?'

"'I am saying that given the way I have been repaid by her daughter, these things do not matter,' Dad replied. 'I was just doing my duty, it turns out. My cover has been blown. Now it is clear that all I did, I did out of convenience. Those were not random acts of goodness done out of love. That would explain why my expected rewards have not been forthcoming.'

"'Mr. Louis, please stop beating up on yourself like that,' the female officer said. 'It only makes you bitterer. Your wife says things about you that a lot of wives would not say about their husbands even if double-barreled guns were held to their heads. You should hold your head high, because the only person whose opinion should matter to you is by your side.'

"'In all the years we have been married, my wife has not washed her car,' Dad said. 'I do that for her every Sunday if it does not rain or snow.'

"'That is what she said,' the female officer said. 'She also said that her car had never broken down on her.'

"'Housekeeping does not qualify as an act of chivalry,' Dad said. 'Don't all real men perform these duties for their wives?'

"'No, they do not,' the female officer said.

"'If they do not, I feel for them,' Dad said. 'They are cutting their lives short. My wife has always had her own ride. Most women, as a function of their gender, have many places to go, many errands to run, and many things to take care of. Husbands do not have the strength or the patience to help their wives keep up with all these commitments. My wife is a deaconess, but she has never been known to get to church on time. Men are not structured that way. Most men will commit to only a few tasks. And they commit to do them very well and to complete them quickly. If a man who prefers to sit in front of his television watching a ballgame in his work outfit is required to change into street clothes to run his wife here and there on days off from his oil-field job, I bet he would return to the oil field and work for free rather than lose his mind being pulled in different directions at home.

"'My dad was a good provider, and he taught me to do the same. He lived to be ninety-five. I learned at the feet of a master. Therefore, every five years, I pay cash and buy my wife a ten-year-old car in very good condition. That's the reason her car has never broken down. I do almost the same with housing. We have never been evicted. That is because my dad told me not to buy a mansion as my buddies who started their first jobs were doing. He said keeping up with the Joneses could stretch my finances, raise my blood pressure and the stress could kill me at a young age, making my beautiful woman available to other men. I was disappointed that I could not be like my friends, who were putting themselves in new cars and humongous houses. But when I realized that my parents were trying to build me up, not to tear me down, I bought a house I could afford and paid it off in no time and then started to build wealth. Not only do we have no mortgage, but we have no debt. We used to have credit cards when the kids were small so that if we needed to travel, we could rent vehicles. Right now, if we cannot pay cash for a purchase, we do not make it. I have since cut our credit cards.'

"'Your record speaks for itself, Mr. Louis,' the female officer said. 'We make one only request of you: extend your goodness a little more. Let it cover your daughter and her excesses.'

"'Forget it, ma'am,' Dad said.

"'Why are you so rigid, sir?' the male officer asked.

"'Because every time I look at this woman and that protrusion in her belly, I see my failure as a father,' Dad said. 'I know that my first child not only will never catch up to her contemporaries but has set a bad example for her younger siblings.'

"'Again, let us remind you that your wife thinks of you as a success story and so does this community,' the female officer said. 'Why, then, do you have a contrarian view of yourself?'

"'I know what success looks and smells like,' Dad said. 'Success has an unmistakable aroma. It is not a feeling. When you see it, you recognize it. A successful father is one whose children look up to and emulate him. Such a father can vouch for his kids because they always let him know that they are involved in positive activities, ones he would not be ashamed of. He can trust them because they have earned his trust. On the other hand, a failed father is one who is called after midnight to post bail to get his kids out of jail and who has a pregnant daughter at home when she should be obtaining a high school diploma.'

"'We all have challenges, Mr. Louis, but we also have hopes to fall back on,' the female officer said. 'That is the reason we do not allow the details of our tasks to overwhelm us. No parent is a 100 percent success story. Raising kids is very much like balancing several moving wheels on different planes. It is not an easy task. Any parent who claims otherwise is either a bald-faced liar or has only been paying child support and has never been involved in the tedious process of raising a child.'

"'Officers, I am sure that as you drove up here, you noticed people in their front yards, esplanades, and cul-de-sacs,' Dad said. 'Do you know who those people were? Those were people who last October rented tillers, prepared the grounds, bought soil and fertilizer, and planted bluebonnet seeds. Now the hard work those people put in has paid off. Those hard-to-cultivate, finicky flowers have blossomed to the delight of passersby. So those gardeners stand around receiving adulation and thanks from friends and the public for a job well done. Success is the reward for success. By the same token, we are now in the season when many dads look forward to seeing their kids put a decent distance between themselves and poverty by heading out to College Station, Duke University, Texas College, Tulane, and Vanderbilt. But what does my child do? She wants to fail so badly that she gets pregnant for a criminal to convince me of her desire. Please persuade her to go somewhere else. As I told you earlier, I do not want to lose my temper, strike her with my palm, and end up being charged with double homicide.'

"'Mr. Louis, falling is not the same thing as failure,' the female officer said. 'Yes, your child failed to reach the goals you set for her and drummed into her all her life. But she has not run out of time for a course correction. The adage says that if you try and do not succeed, to try and try again. Second chances are not unheard of in these parts. Your daughter is young. She has the time and the energy to try again. Do not deny her the chance.'

"'Officers, that type of unrealistic optimism is the reason people fail miserably at their assigned tasks,' Dad said. 'They assume, without evidence, that they are so important to providence that they have time on their side, that they will be permitted to take their sweet time to accomplish their tasks. That is a wrong assumption. Time waits for no one. William Shakespeare correctly said, "Fate, show thy force. Ourselves we do not owe." Therefore, it is foolish to think that you control time instead of the other way round.

"'Talking about adages, I prefer the one that says it may take just one person to lead a cow to a stream, but if upon getting to the water, the cow decides it is not thirsty, even if several villagers band together to hold down its head, they won't be able to make that cow take a drink. If those people keep trying to force the cow to drink, it will kick and they will discover to their dismay that sometimes wills and ways are not one and the same thing.

"'I am not up to date on modern science and the gadgets great minds are inventing and insisting everyone must have, but there are certain telltale signs that have had the same message since I was a kid. One of them is that when an underage girl gets pregnant, that is usually an indication that she does not want to be associated with a place of learning. And since science has also shown that an American kid needs at least a high school education to stave off poverty, I can never be reconciled with any child of mine who places more value on a GED than I place on a high school diploma and a college degree. Perpetuating poverty is a deal breaker for me. I'm out of here,' Dad said as he went into the master bedroom to pack a suitcase.

"'Wait up, Mr. Louis,' the male officer said. Dad stopped and listened.

"'Mr. Louis, if nature itself has made room to accommodate the mistakes that will undoubtedly accompany life, why can't we, imperfect creations, despite being made in the image of a perfect Creator, make allowance for a comeback by those we love even after they have offended us grievously?'

"'I am sorry, officers,' Dad said. 'I am not a puzzle guru. I do not have the answer to that riddle.'

"'Take a stab at it,' the officer said.

"'Thank you, sir,' Dad said, 'but I do not have time for that. I need to find a place to sleep tonight. I am no longer welcome in my own house.'

"'Well, I think there is a reason that not every mistake we make is fatal,' the female officer said.

"'You are right,' Dad said, 'but don't you have to admit to the mistake first? If you do not admit to your mistakes, you see no reason to make amends. Most likely, you will be encouraged to offend more. Humans tend to do more of the things that cost them nothing. On the other hand, even nature does not see the need for forgiveness if an offender keeps on offending. That is why serpents have no legs.

"'You all heard what this little punk said to me in my house. He is not willing to make a commitment to his unpaid whore and latest concubine. He said he is an independent contractor not bound by commitments. I hate to admit it, but the punk is right. My child did not have him sign a statement of commitment to her and their child. The gigolo is in the business of sowing wild oats—nothing personal, he told you. He has already made so many babies, so what is the big deal about making another one under my nose? He is not willing to make a commitment to his child. Since my wife sees nothing wrong with this picture, we have nothing to work with. I'm out of here.'

"'Mr. Louis, please stay. You are the undisputed head of this family. Do not worsen a bad situation. Your family needs its high priest. That is you," the female officer said.

"'Ma'am, you do not wish me well,' Dad said, 'but I wish my family well. That is the reason I have to leave. If I stay to deal with this mess, I will start drinking. That would be much more destructive, not just to me but to the little ones who are the reason for my living. As they used to say in the days of reel-to-reel films, this is the end.'"

CHAPTER 6

MARY HAD TWIN girls exactly ten months after she gave birth to her first child. Despite the additional mouths to feed, Frank Perry was in no hurry to find a job. His excuse was that hiring managers did not like him. He said that potential employers, often white men, discriminated against him by running background checks on him. He said discrimination was the reason his applications never got a second look.

Mrs. Louis asked people who owed her favors to help her find a job for Perry. Most of them told her that his appearance made hiring him look risky. They said she should suggest to him that he look for work in the oil fields, where even an ex-convict with too many tattoos and body piercings and without a high school diploma could find work and make decent money. Perry rejected the idea, saying work in the oil fields was too hard and that he did not want to cut his dreads.

She mulled over putting her little grandbabies in day care and falsifying their mother's birth certificate so she could look for a job, but after she tabulated the weekly cost of day care and how much her daughter might be making working entry-level jobs, she concluded that it was more cost effective for Mary to stay home and take care of her babies than to outsource their care.

Mrs. Louis asked her employer for more overtime hours. When she could not get as many as she needed, she took a second job across town. But standing on her feet all day at the two jobs was killing her slowly despite the high doses of pain reliever she took before and after work. Her back hurt. Her knees hurt. Her ankles swelled and hurt badly, but she could not afford to slow down. She had no one to complain to or to ask for a little help.

After Mr. Louis got pushed out of his house by Mary's pregnancy, Mrs. Louis called for a meeting with her daughter and Perry. She pointed out that because Mary was underage and Perry had a criminal background, neither of them could get jobs to help her pay household bills. Therefore, she informed them that she had decided to move the flower shop she and her husband owned. She was moving it from a flea market to a more visible storefront location and to have the two of them run it. She did not give them the option of refusing to go along with her plan.

Mrs. Louis took a two-week, unpaid vacation from her main job and used the time to set up the store. The shop included a small nursery in the back, and she put a playpen behind the display counter.

Her daughter and Perry received on-the-job training. Mrs. Louis ordered them audio books to study the basics of the flower business, customer service, processing credit transactions, and keeping a driving log for tax purposes. She also put them in touch with suppliers and large-order customers like corporations, hospitals, and funeral homes. After the setup was done, she stayed behind the scenes while the two ran the shop. When she was satisfied that they had everything down pat, Mrs. Louis returned to her job at the hospital. But every morning before she left her car with them, she reminded Perry that since he did not have a valid driver's license and the insurance on the car did not cover him, he should not roam the streets with the vehicle. She begged him to drive carefully and to use the car only for flower deliveries. Every morning she sat her daughter and Perry down and repeated these instructions, which she called the standing order. Then she would ride a bus to work.

At night, after leaving her second job, Mrs. Louis would catch a bus for the store, not just to pick up her car but to examine the books, to fill out sales-tax papers, and to inspect the shop, which was always sloppy. She was a neat freak, and so she always made sure everything was in order for the next business day. For instance, she would arrange all the paid orders in the cooler according to delivery times.

She was not terribly disappointed that all the cleaning was left to her. However, she was upset that Perry was ignoring other chores she had instructed him to do, such as filling out the driving log to satisfy an Internal Revenue Service requirement.

Mrs. Louis was also concerned about how quickly her car was looking like a piece of junk. Perry was not using it according to her stipulations. The car's interior, which her husband delighted in keeping immaculate, brought tears to her eyes. It looked like the inside of a trash compactor at a fast-food joint. The carpet and the seats were smeared with syrup, fruit juice, jelly, and other gooey stuff. Underneath and between the seats, she found brittle French fries, moldy hamburger buns, and hairy meat patties. The steering wheel was so sticky that she would have to stay up all night cleaning with soapy water and a steel brush to get out the grunge. She kept winter gloves in the trunk so she could handle the steering wheel. Driving home, she had to roll down the windows and turn off the AC to keep from choking on the mix of cigarette smoke and incense trapped in the vehicle. The only good news was that the store was not losing money.

After two months of around-the-clock stress from running between her jobs and the store, Mrs. Louis thought that since the store was at least breaking even, she should give up her second job and focus on working at the shop on weekends. Her vendors had asked her to increase her offerings since her store was located in an underserved part of the city. They invited her to a florist convention to discuss help with expanding her business. The convention conflicted with her work schedule, so she called her husband and asked to meet. He refused and hung up. She thought about the good life they had had together and about the years she had invested in their relationship and concluded that she did not deserve to be treated this way. She located the motel where her husband was staying and surprised him. When she knocked on his door, he looked through the peephole and came out to meet her in the hallway.

"Hey, baby. It is so good to see you."

"Yeah, yeah. What planet is this? What's up?" he asked.

"In a couple of weeks I will need you to do me a huge favor. Would you?"

"No, but I am listening."

"Flowers of America, the umbrella trade group for American florists, is having its next convention in Dallas in a little more than a month."

"And what has that got to do with me?"

She asked if he could attend the business meeting in her stead or keep an eye on the store while she was at the convention. He asked where her daughter and the daughter's drug-addicted boyfriend would be. She said they would be at the store, working side by side with him.

"I think you've got me mixed up with somebody who is suicidal," Mr. Louis said.

"When and how did I do that?" Mrs. Louis asked.

He told her he did not want to be involved in their disastrous lives and would never go near the shop. Not only did Perry remain a thorn in his side and Mary an affront to his standards, Mr. Louis said, but the two represented a clear and present danger to him. He said he would never be around them for any reason.

"Let me tell you this: One of these days the punks who are crazier than Perry and to whom he owes drug money will show up at the shop with military-style weapons. They will shoot up the place. I have no intention of being around when those avengers come for Perry's blood and their money."

"Honey, why are you so pessimistic?"

"Good day, ma'am," he said, doing an about-face and returning to his room. He did not realize until he tried to shut the door that his wife was right behind him.

"Baby, may I come in, please?" Mrs. Louis asked her husband.

"No," he said.

"Pretty please, honey," she said.

"No, ma'am."

"Come on, baby."

"Why?"

"I am your wife," she said. He hesitated.

"Why?"

"I said that I am your wife."

"Yeah, but why are you still my wife, seeing that we have nothing in common anymore? We are incompatible." He waited to hear the real reason for her request to enter the room. She shrugged but stood in the doorway and insisted on being let in. He had been married to her long enough to recognize that her stance meant she was not leaving anytime soon. He relented and let her walk past him into the room.

Mrs. Louis surveyed the room carefully as if she were a sanitation inspector checking up on a restaurant that had been cited for serving food that made customers sick. She made a mental note of the peeling paint on the walls, the worn carpet, the dust caked on the ceiling fan, and the unmistakable smell of bedding that had had close contact with scores of sweaty, naked bodies over a long period.

"I cannot believe that you, Mr. Clean, have allowed yourself to live here all these months you have been away from your family. Why do you stay in this sickening dump when you could have gotten a decent apartment at a lesser price?"

"This is my little heaven."

"That is pure blasphemy and you know it."

"I have peace of mind here."

"No, you do not," she said.

"Yes, I do," he replied forcefully.

"How can you? This place is toxic even to that steel desk and chair over there. It has to be unhealthy for any organism whose life depends on breathing oxygen."

"If the place ends up killing me, it will be over a period of time, and I would have been long gone by then. My chances of my being alive are better here than at the shop where some drug addict could empty his weapon and kill me in an instant. Besides, I don't have to be here all the time, so the place can't be that unhealthy."

Mrs. Louis noticed the cigarette burns on the carpet. She could not stand the smell of the secondhand smoke coming from the floor and infiltrating her clothes. Maybe the smell came from raw sewage, she thought. She felt faint. She tried to open a window and found that it was stuck. She opened the door to a tiny bathroom. She walked in and quickly walked out.

"Baby, I am much more puzzled about you now than before."

"Why is that?"

"I could have sworn that you had a woman in here, but you don't."

"Have you checked the hall closet?"

"There is no hall closet or anything remotely resembling one in this matchbox."

"Damn," Mr. Louis said.

"Honey, you have a home waiting for you. You abandoned it to be here. I could see the reason if you had a bimbo you needed to squirrel away, but you don't. Give me the real reason for this very out-of-character behavior of yours. Why do you live in this burrow? Is it just to make a point?"

"I did not make the decision. You made it for me. I merely granted your wish."

"I thought we were a team."

"I mistakenly thought we were more than that."

"You're right, baby. We were tight."

"We were tighter than a turtle in its shell. That was what your dad wanted. He told me that your heart belonged to him and that if I broke it, I would answer to him. He begged me not to give him a reason to use the shotgun in his pickup truck."

"Yes, we were a team, and I could not have asked for a better teammate. Other boys tried to talk to me, but I chose you because my friends thought you were so together, so mature for your years. All your actions were so grown-up and thought through. Remember how, instead of hanging out and drinking with our friends at bars, we would go to the park and sit down with a pencil and paper to map out our life together? We started out as a team and remained a team, baby."

"A team that opposes itself ceases to qualify as a team. If we were a team, why did you undermine my authority?"

"Honey, I love you with all my being. How did I undermine your authority as the king of our castle?"

"You undermined me all the time and not subtly but openly, just to prove you were the friendlier parent."

"Oh baby, name me one instance."

"Are you sure that you have the time? I could write a book on this topic."

"Try me."

"All right. We agreed that our children should not do sleepovers, but as soon as my back was turned, you allowed them. We decided that except for field trips chaperoned by school officials we knew, our children would not go anywhere without one of us accompanying them. We had agreed that they would not ride school buses, instead that we would drop them off and pick them up from school and that when they were old enough to safely operate autos, I would be the one to teach our kids to drive. But without informing me, you paid for your daughter to take driving classes."

"That was because she was feeling left out, like an outcast. All her friends were driving and she was not."

"You had forgotten that I told you automobiles are dangerous weapons in the hands of preteens and teenagers. There have been numerous stories about young people unknowingly driving their friends to commit crimes, not to talk of accidents. I did not want my child to end up in the criminal justice system."

"Honey, I have always told our daughter to be careful when driving."

"We also agreed that it was not an invasion of privacy for us to randomly and without warning lock down our kids and their spaces to assure ourselves that they were not involved with drugs, alcohol, or body piercing. We agreed that they would never get tattoos but would always be well-groomed, respectful, and respectable, since appearance is very important in job situations. What about dating? Did we not agree that since we were not planning on raising grandkids, our kids would not date until they were done with high school? What did you do? You kept me in the dark when my daughter not only began to date but brought a tattoo-covered drug addict to my house for the nasty."

"Okay, baby, my drum major and scorekeeper, points taken. Now come back to your home. We need you."

"That is not going to happen, not in this lifetime. You are now the sole captain of the ship. I will never be back at the helm. Steer it your way. My demanding ways are a thing of the past. Go celebrate. You have won. In your view, I was too strict, suffocating your daughter. Now she can have all the freedom her heart desires. Good-bye."

"Honey, why are you abandoning all your children for the mistake of one? That's like tossing out into a dumpster a ten-pound bag of apples on account of one bad apple."

"What do you mean that I am abandoning my children?" Mr. Louis asked. "I have already taught the ones who were paying attention all the lessons they will need for the rest of their lives. As my folks used to say, in the first five years of life a child acquires every tool he will ever need, and as he grows, all he has to do is revisit those life lessons and he will be okay. We need not reinvent the wheel. And besides, I have been making child-support payments to you. I will continue to send checks until all our kids leave for college or become adults. Have you not been getting the checks I have been sending?"

"Whatever! Our kids need their dad at home with them."

"I do not know about that!"

"Yes they do, honey. What they do not need is an absentee dad mailing them handouts from this place of ill repute. I know you have an agenda that you hold close to your heart, but return home where you belong, baby."

"That is impossible. That option is no longer on the table. How many times do I have to repeat that?"

"Or at least move out of this working-girls' headquarters to a decent apartment where the kids who have not unforgivably offended you can go see their dad without being propositioned by pimps."

"That won't be necessary."

"It is very necessary."

"No, it's not."

"What are you talking about, baby?"

"I'm getting ready to ship out of here even as we speak."

"Thank God for that."

"That's right. I'm going overseas."

"You can't be serious."

"Yes, I am. I am as serious as death. You know that I have always made money the old-fashioned way. That has worked to a certain extent. I have provided for my family. But now that my family has left me behind, it's time to test my luck. I am going to try something very different."

"Are you going to become a drug mule? I know you have not asked my advice for a while, but I would say do not be a drug courier. Two things are working against you. Number one, due to knee and ankle injuries you picked up in the oil field, you can't run as fast as you used to. That means you won't be able to outrun the police.

"Number two, when you are locked up, the jailhouse is neither equipped nor required by court order to give you your medications at the exact time you are supposed to take them. Sometimes corrections officers must handle situations or paperwork and forget to give inmates their medications. So for men with chronic diseases there is the real possibility of dying in prison."

"I have no chronic disease. You know that."

"I know for a fact that you are on special eye drops to lower the pressure in your right eye. You are taking or should be taking medication for high blood pressure and for your diabetic neuropathy. This is not a good time for you to get locked up for trying to peddle a few kilos of illegal drugs."

"Thanks for your concern, but you have nothing to worry about. I am not going abroad to do anything criminal or even mildly stupid. But I confess that the chance to make a six-figure salary is making me high. John put in a good word and landed me a job with a resupply boat. That is the reason I am not always here. I have been attending offshore training classes here and in Louisiana. I am getting a transportation worker ID card, a merchant marine license, a crane operator's license, and a helicopter pass. As soon as I am done with all these certifications, it's bye-bye America for at least 365 days. I can't wait to finally make that six-figure salary. I postponed it long enough to raise my family.

"Now that my first child and her mom have brought to my attention that I am nothing but a fifth leg on a four-legged table, I need to hurry up and make some money before I get too old to pass the stringent physicals required of all Americans seeking to work abroad."

"I knew there was a woman involved," Mrs. Louis said. "Where, when, and how?"

"What's her name and where does she come from? Do not play dumb with me. Your buddy John Gold-leaf went overseas. After working there for a year, he thought he was rich. He returned home with enough money to pay off his house and other debts. Along the way, he suddenly discovered that his wife was not just old but was not submissive enough to him. But being a good man, he had sympathy for this old woman. He compensated her with a new car for being a good mom to his kids. Then he divorced her and married a woman from the Philippines whom he met overseas. Your other buddy, James Brownie, took it a step further. Unlike John, James did not just marry a submissive woman and bring her home. No. After marrying a submissive woman, he moved to the Philippines with her, buying riverfront properties in her name. With your competitive nature, I suppose you are going to top your buddies' amorous performances. You are going to find a young Kenyan woman who is dying to come to America to make you another set of babies. That would make you young again."

"So you feel that I am not going abroad to make money but to meet babes and to make babies."

"Damn straight!" Mrs. Louis said.

"Interesting! I wish I had thought about that before my strength diminished. Are you willing to bet money?"

"Yes."

"No, seriously, I am flattered that your research shows I am going abroad for the same reason normal, middle-aged American males go into debt to put themselves in expensive sports cars. Your contention is that I am trying to show I've still got it, right?"

"That is right. You are, after all, a military man. Posture is very important to you. That is the reason you deliberately walk erect as you walked when you were in your twenties and in active service. What does that tell you?"

"I do not know. You are the expert here. What does it tell me?"

"That like most men born after the Second World War, the so called Young Urban Professionals or Yuppies, you are in denial not just about the aging process but about age itself. Some of you get into debt by buying yuppie mobiles. Others acquire new and younger women and start raising families all over again. Therefore, even when your backs and your knees, as with most men in their fifties, hurt like crazy, you bear with the pain. You do not stop and take a break when you feel the need to do so. You have convinced yourself that you are younger than you feel. Now you are going to convince the world that you are still virile and are not a frumpy, balding guy with excess stomach hanging over his belt. A trophy wife in a house filled with the sound of little feet will make that declaration loudly without your uttering a word. That has been your goal all along. Prove me wrong. Leave this dump and move back with your family, the family that you have invested so much in, a family that loves you dearly."

"Then put your money where your mouth is!"

"I do not have any money, and you know it."

"I do not know if I am allowed to speak in my own defense at this hastily convened court-martial, but my love for you and for your children never ended. It was not out there, searching for a place to go. It had already reached its destination. It had settled. It was no longer susceptible to being tossed about. Even in my private moments, I was not furtively looking around for greener pastures. Just like my dad and my grandparents before me, I believe in one set of parents for one set of kids. But if the measure of how much I love my daughter is my willingness to take a bullet in the head for the foolish choices she defiantly makes, then I must draw the line. But let the record show that I have been loyal to this family."

"Yeah, you were all of those things until a little trial and temptation appeared."

"You and I are different in one respect. Unlike African elementary school teachers, I am not patient enough to wait for my reward in heaven. Therefore, I cannot call a major revolution 'a little trial and temptation.' What yardstick are you using? My parents died in their nineties. With the living arrangement you have approved for your house, if I move back there, my life span will be drastically reduced. If I move back, I may not have two years left on earth. So whether you believe it or not, my going abroad serves two crucial purposes for me. First, it puts a lot of tax-free money in my bank account so I can support any of my kids who wants to go to college and to have a life instead of running on the streets. Second, this trip will shield me from bullets meant for somebody else in your house. As for any other motive, you can rest easy."

"Yeah, right!"

"If you had money, I would say place a bet and lose the money to me: I am not going overseas to find a maiden. If that had been my intention at any point, I would not have waited here and toiled for this family this long—until the warranties on most of my original equipment had run out. As you know very well, my hearing, sight, and memory are now operating at reduced capacities. Why would I find another woman and risk starting another family at a time like this?"

"I am the first to say that you have been a good provider, but sometimes you were mean to our kids because they didn't measure up to the Mayfield children. You have no obligation to be anybody else but your kids' father. If you have anything to prove, it is that you can love your children unconditionally."

"Okay, why did it take you so long to give me this performance evaluation? Up to now, you never complained that I was parenting in the wrong way. I did what I thought would benefit my family. To insist that my daughter live a purpose-driven life is not being too hard on her. To insist that babies should not be having babies is not exactly setting civilization back. To insist that a child not be sexually active until she has enough wisdom not to allow her body to be abused is not hard-hearted. It is for her own good.

"Moses recounts how one of the Jewish patriarchs severely punished his firstborn child, his own heir, for the son's sexual impropriety. That shows us that immorality should neither be covered up nor tolerated. Parents should not economize on discipline. That's what you're asking me to do. I refuse. As parents, we should support each other in increasing the cost of aberrant behavior in our kids. We should never decrease that cost. If we do, we upset the proper balance in the upbringing of our progeny and contribute to the overcrowding of the jailhouses."

"Honey, you have been too hard on her. That is not a criticism but an honest-to-goodness truth. You should realize that kids these days have too much happening in their young lives. As a consequence, they do not have the time to live by the hard and fast rules we were raised on. Such rules make kids doubt themselves. The way we grew up was stifling. Just ask any child psychologist."

"You know quite well that I have never made the acquaintance of any."

"You should because they have something to say about family dynamics that you do not understand. There is a reason kids refer to us as old school. Psychologists agree with them, not with us."

"That is the problem. These people's relevance comes from the number of book they peddle. The champions of self-esteem pride themselves on being seen as friends instead of parents to their kids. They oppose those of us who believe that childhood is a time for learning and that the future belongs to kids with moral compasses for the journey ahead."

"Baby, listen. Good leaders set themselves apart not just by goose-stepping forward but by constantly making sure they are not too far ahead of their followers. Good leaders strive to get feedback from those they lead. That benefits everyone. If leaders keep marching ahead without looking back, they may not know when a weak follower needs help or when to nip a mutiny in the bud. That is what child psychologists are worried about."

"You and I noticed how it worked for the rich people who employed our parents. We decided that this arrangement would work for us. You became a stay-at-home mom. It was hard at first, but I worked my butt off to provide for my family. Sometimes we were way behind on our bills, but we always had a place to stay. We never ended up on the streets. When you rejoined the workforce, that decision was yours alone. I did not ask you to."

"Yes, honey. You are so right, but since we were a team, I thought that was the right thing to do. I wanted to help any way I could."

"I believe you noticed that I did not slack off even though you were bringing in a check. No, I kept busting my behind. Though we did not own expensive automobiles and take expensive vacations, I thought we were doing just fine."

"You are right. We always had lights at our house, air conditioning in the summer, and heat in the winter. And we always had each other. I was hoping we would grow old together. But now it looks like some African woman whom you have had on layaway for years, worried about her biological clock, is beckoning you from across the Atlantic Ocean to come to her if she can't come to you anytime soon."

"I do not need to tell you this, but you know that I had planned for our marriage to go the distance."

"And that was so reassuring to me, baby. For years, I walked on air. Wherever I looked, the evidence was clear. Most women did not have what I had," Mrs. Louis said.

"In appreciation, you permitted my daughter to be a wayward child. As if that was not enough, you looked the other way when a punk with a mouth full of fake gold teeth violated the sanctity of my home. Were you doing those things to protest my autocratic rule?"

"No, I was not."

"Well, correct me if I am wrong, but were you not aware when immorality and defiance arose in my house? Did you tell me what you knew and when you knew about it?"

"Well, you …"

"The answer is that you definitely did not. Telling me, even after all the major damage had been done, in your estimation would have been too unfriendly to the kids. So why not keep the spoiler in the dark, eh? My position regarding discipline will never be a crowd pleaser. You in the self-esteem business have already cornered the popularity market. I do not want any part of it. You are angels, while we who insist on boundaries are forever monsters to our kids."

"I have never and will never label you a monster. But I wish you had not focused entirely on discipline like your mentor Mr. Mayfield, who believed religiously that a child always takes a yard upon being given an inch."

"Stop blaming Mr. Mayfield. The man is a professional, and he was right in saying that childhood is the time in life when the brain is supposed to do what is designed to do, which is to learn. He said that in childhood the brain is like a sponge, absorbing efficiently and without effort. Therefore, he said that we should not let our kids pass their time in idleness or in learning anything that would not add to their living a life of purpose.

"I am a testament to the fact that a time comes when the brain takes a vacation. So learning, whether it is how to cook or how to do algebra must be done when the brain is not heading out on a sabbatical. As I said, look at me.

"In my youth, when I served in South Korea, I learned the Korean language with little effort. In California, I picked up Mandarin the same way. But now that I need to understand enough Spanish to order food at authentic Spanish restaurants, old age won't let me. My brain is on vacation. It is not willing to come out of retirement to work with me. Despite all the night classes I have taken and the numerous books I have purchased, my Spanish is still limited to days of the week and the numbers one to twenty. I am handicapped that way. Our children should not be. You should have stood with me and insisted that learning come first.

"Yes, I am jealous of Mr. Mayfield. He has succeeded enormously with all his kids while I have fallen on my face with mine, but do not confuse him with my dad. My parents taught me versatility. I wanted to pass that on to my kids. My parents taught me not to hang all my career hopes on one job. You know that I have been a certified welder, a small-engine mechanic, a forklift operator, a crane operator, and a truck driver. My parents pushed me to learn all these trades in preparation for doing any work that pays money.

"Do you remember my cousin Roswell? He was so good a running back that everyone bet he would not only be drafted to play for the American National Football Federation but would be the federation's ambassador and sell American football to the 95 percent of the world addicted to soccer. That talented cousin lost his kneecap in his final year in college and was never drafted to play professionally. He had no other skills. Growing up, he knew and learned only football. My dad theorized that if his nephew could not be guaranteed a career in what he loved to do and was very good at doing maybe I should expand my options.

"As for this child who has so shamed me, remember that from the time she was in grade school, I never failed to tell her to avoid boys seeking to pull her down. She flouted my authority. She is lucky she has lived to tell about it. I resigned as a father to her. I will not come back to that house, because I am not a dog that returns to its vomit. Good-bye."

CHAPTER 7

Mrs. Louis was at the business convention in Dallas, Texas, when she received a phone call to come home ASAP. She was afraid to ask why she was needed in such a hurry. Whatever the problem, she could not leave the convention immediately. She had carpooled with a bunch of people who had no intention of leaving before the event was properly adjourned with a mouth-watering dinner.

In the past, her husband used to chauffeur her to and fro on out-of-town trips like this one, but since that option was no longer available and she did not trust herself not to fall asleep behind the steering wheel, she had caught a ride with other convention attendees from Houston. Now that she needed to head back home as soon as possible, she could not. She called Statewide Coach Transportation, but the bus company said it did not have a bus going to Houston until the next day. She called a cab company. A dispatcher was nice enough to tell her it would be cheaper for her to rent a car than to charter a taxi to take her to Houston. She was stuck until the convention ran its course.

When the carpool arrived in Houston, Mrs. Louis asked to be dropped off at her flower shop. She knew no one would be there at that hour, but she went inside and looked around. The place was as filthy as she had expected it would be. Some floral arrangements had been paid for and should have been delivered to funeral homes but were not. She suppressed the urge to worry about why those deliveries were not made. She also suppressed the urge to undertake the Herculean task of tidying up the place. She turned off the lights, lowered the blinds, locked the doors, and was out of there.

Mrs. Louis got into her car. The dashboard and the steering wheel were as sticky as she expected. She popped open the glove compartment to get her gloves so she could handle the sticky steering wheel, and she noticed an object that looked like a brick inside. What would a brick be doing in there? She took it out and examined it closely. It was not as heavy as a brick. She sniffed it and determined that it was a stack of greenbacks.

What would a stack of greenbacks be doing in the glove compartment of her car? She returned the money to the glove compartment, looked behind her, backed out of the parking space, and headed home.

As Mrs. Louis turned into her driveway, she noticed a bunch of neighbors whom she knew only by sight talking to police officers on the curb near her front yard. She was afraid to stop and ask what brought them there, but she had a feeling that something bad had taken place. She activated the garage door opener mounted on the visor of her car, her dread growing as she inched the automobile into the garage. No one in the house seemed to notice she was home. She looked for Mary and the babies and found them along with her other children huddled in Mary's room with the lights turned off.

"Hello," she said, turning on the lights. None of the kids ran toward her. Mary began to cry, shaking violently like someone suffering a violent bout of malarial fever.

"What is going on?" Mrs. Louis asked. No one seemed to have heard the question. "Somebody, please talk to me."

"Momma, they killed my Frankie," Mary said.

"What are you talking about?"

"Momma, my Frankie is dead."

"What do you mean Frank is dead?"

"Some guys came into the flower shop in the afternoon and spoke with him. I was busy with a customer and couldn't hear what their conversation was about. They all went outside. After a while, I heard a pop, pop, pop sound. After a while, I went outside to ask Frankie to make a delivery. I saw him in a pool of blood. Momma, in broad daylight they had shot and killed him right outside the shop, yet no one called the police."

"No, no, no. Frank cannot be dead, not right now. He cannot leave behind all this mess for me. Your father was right. You have bought yourself a boatload of trouble."

****

To get Mary out of her funk, the supervising nurse had spent precious company time reliving her own life as well as Mary's. She did not realize how long she had been in the bathroom providing therapy until the supervising nurse for the next shift came in, looking for her. She returned to her desk to finish her paperwork and to get her purse. From there, she and Mary went to the break room to clock out. She offered Mary a ride home, but as they were leaving the building, someone honked at them. Mary turned around and saw Emmanuel waving at her.

"I've been waiting for you," he hollered.

Mary told her supervisor that she had a ride.

"Good catch, sister. Life is meant to be lived. I say live it to the fullest. Do not cut it short, no matter how hard you think it is," her supervisor told her.

"No, he is just a friend," Mary said.

"Whatever. Go ahead. Run along. Remember to live life to the fullest."

Mary thanked her for providing a shoulder to cry on and for letting her keep her job.

CHAPTER 8

"**H**ELLO, MARY."

"Hey, Emmanuel!"

"How was your day?"

"Not good at all."

"Oh? What happened?"

"Because of what happened at the school, life held no attraction for me. The only good thing about today was that despite not putting in a lick of work, I did not get fired."

"Praise the Lord."

"I was wrong about my supervisor. As they say, it's not good to judge a book by its cover. My supervisor is a good person."

"Thank God for his favor. He gives everyone a worth. No human is totally useless."

"I also know it was a bad day for you."

"What makes you say that, Mary?" Emmanuel asked with alarm.

"Why did you not correct me long ago?"

"Correct you about what?"

"I found out from my supervisor that Rose is not your sister but your wife."

"No kidding!" Emmanuel said.

"You know that I am not a nurse but a nurse aide. That means any good gossip making the rounds of this psychiatric hospital does not reach me on a timely basis, if at all. By the time I hear a tale it is no longer juicy but desiccated. But let me ask you this. If you are not Rose's brother but her husband and she does not have a brother anywhere in the United States, who is this guy who has been calling the unit so incessantly, asking for her?"

"I want to know the answer to that question as well. I hope you are the person who can help me solve that puzzle."

Emmanuel did not want to admit it, but he had known for a while that Rose did not care about him. He had tried to sound spiritual in order not to look completely dumb and weak to the people who could not wait to say, "I told you so." His increasingly spiritual tone also helped him to rationalize that love was a slow-growing plant and that the only way to make it blossom was to look the other way while watering it with tears, patience, self-denial, and hope. He accepted the one-sidedness of love in this situation as karma for the way he had treated the loving and helpful American saint he had dated for years. Emmanuel had asked her to terminate several pregnancies, but one resulted in a baby he had forgotten to mention to his parents.

After her dad had said he did not appreciate having his daughter strung along, Emmanuel had married the girl. But because he had determined in his heart that the marriage was not for real, he changed from being the lovable man the girl had been proud to introduce and became cruel, criticizing everything about her from her weight to her hygiene. Then he divorced her.

The baggage remained. Emmanuel had succeeded in forgetting about that marriage and had concentrated on his African import. However, in quiet moments alone with himself, he mused that he had no right to expect to have a happy, fruitful relationship with any woman, given the way he had used and abandoned the American girl. His friends had called her promiscuous, and he had done nothing to correct them. Foreign men like him often married young and unsuspecting American women in order to stay in the country. As a former seminarian, Emmanuel knew this was wrong, making a mockery of a sacrament. He realized he had destroyed another person's life and future to build his, and he prayed his sin would not find him out. As a lifelong Roman Catholic, he hoped that Rose's lack of love for him was his penance for the sin of his sham marriage. Emmanuel hoped that Rose would eventually love him as he loved her, particularly after she had lived in America and been in the workforce long enough to appreciate the financial sacrifice he had made to bring her to the United States.

Rose was making her husband's time in purgatory more hellish than he had feared. Every day friends would hear her say outrageous things about him. They kept their cool. But after they noticed her act in ways contrary to a good marriage, they took action. They drew Emmanuel's attention to this behavior. He would say something to put those friends at ease. It was not clear if he was at ease himself, but he did not want his friends to know that Rose's plans did not include him.

CHAPTER 9

ROSE HAD NEVER flown in an airplane before being brought to America. Though she did not tell her husband and sponsor, she was grateful to Providence for her unusual luck. But even before she boarded the Nigerian Airways flight, paid for with Emmanuel's sweat, on the first leg of her trip out of Nigeria, she did not pretend to love him or care about him. Everyone except Emmanuel could see that.

In post-civil war Nigeria, young people, even the privileged ones, were raised to love and respect the parents of their spouses with the same intensity they did their own parents. Rose was different. She never curtsied or bowed on seeing her husband's parents. That was an early sign that Emmanuel should not have missed. However, he suffered from a modern American disease, attention deficit disorder. That's what his people concluded after observing that Emmanuel was not alarmed when Rose did not hang around his parents. His cousins did not mince words when they told him she was laying the groundwork to leave him for another man upon reaching America. Rose did not try to prove them wrong. But after arriving in the United States and discovering the high cost of living, she had to put her plan to jump ship on hold. She let Emmanuel take care of her.

While she was taking pre-nursing classes, her accent and her strong, bony African face drew attention. Rose was sought out by a bunch of militant former layaway wives whose relationships with the African men who brought them to America were beyond repair. They hung around and ate lunch together, building each other up. They were outraged when they found out that Rose's husband had pushed her into a nursing career just as their former husbands did with them. They cursed him for bringing a young, extremely beautiful girl to the United States to work in nursing homes. Had she remained in Africa, they believed, she would undoubtedly have caught the eye of a prime minister or a finance minister and became the next wife to either or both.

The former layaway wives forcibly opened Rose's eyes and enlightened her. They provided her with solid evidence that her no-good husband brought her to America to be his workhorse so he could keep running back to Africa to invest her money in losing businesses instead of getting a real job in a robust American economy like Asian and European men did. The women consoled Rose with the thought that every step she took to avenge her husband's injustice was a justifiable act of self-preservation.

They advised her not to feel guilty but to avoid the mistakes they had made after being brought over in slave ships to America. She corrected them, saying she had escaped Nigeria during military rule and had fled by airplane. They countered that they knew what they were talking about. All she needed to do was listen to them like a schoolgirl receiving wisdom at the feet of her elders.

They pointed out to Rose a heinous act of injustice done her. When she departed Nigeria, there were nonstop Concorde flights to America and other luxurious airliners with first-class amenities as well. Those planes left Nigeria weekly. Her husband had let this beautiful girl endure the humiliation of flying Nigerian Airways, which for some ominous reason was symbolized by an elephant, an animal that didn't fly, and this called for reprisals with no room for reconciliation.

The charter members of the association of former layaway wives cautioned Rose against making babies with Emmanuel just because he had paid for her passage to America. They introduced her to a wonderful tool called the migraine headache and showed her how she could employ it to work magic for herself in the house that would soon be hers if she played her cards right. They explained that since she planned to leave her husband for another man, making a baby while still in his custody would be a huge problem. That was because women with kids from previous relationships tended to have little value in a marketplace dominated by African men who had lived too long in America to still qualify as Africans.

After considering the logistics of employing the migraine-headache ruse, Rose asked her handlers how long she could slither away from her husband with the excuse that her head was killing her, given the fact that they shared a bed for upward of eight hours nightly. She also needed a clarification concerning where she would stay if her stinginess prompted her irate husband to kick her out of his house on a rainy night.

The women begged Rose to think positively, if not for herself, then for the thousands of young, pimple-faced virgins whom these old, useless African men living enormous financial clouds would continue to commandeer and bring to America to become trophy wives, baby factories, and cash cows in that order.

As for keeping her husband from an activity they referred to as drilling for oil on what he thought was his private ranch, the women assured Rose there was a way around this. They noted that American nursing schools required students to do free internships at health care facilities to see how the theories taught in classrooms worked in real life. They advised her to volunteer at two facilities, if not more. That way she would be home infrequently or not at all.

Rose took their advice and signed up for her clinical work at a big hospital and at a nursing home simultaneously. The plan worked, to her surprise and to the delight of her handlers. She was rarely home when her husband was there. That was perfect. The house became like a rest-stop on a highway. Rose went there, took a nap, and headed back out. She did not have to feign a migraine or any other ailment to duck what her handlers said only primitive societies considered a wife's natural duty to a husband.

Rose's job situation also provided a cover to push Emmanuel's plan to start a family to the back burner without getting into argument with him. But she wondered how long she could keep up the ruse. During periodic and ongoing consultations to assess her progress, the former layaway wives assured her that it would be to her advantage to keep her husband at bay for at least six months. All she needed to do was to keep working, and if her husband happened to be home when she stopped by to grab a nap, and if he began to act like a he-goat that had just picked up a whiff of a female pheromone, she should nicely but firmly say to him, "Honey, could we do this the next time I am off duty? I have a headache today."

Though they had never met Emmanuel, the women assured Rose that the odds were very good that he was a primitive male chauvinist pig who didn't understand that wives have the right to say no even to their husbands. After she had consistently denied him what he considered his entitlement, they said, this man would most likely become frustrated and angry and hit her, or worse, force himself on her, which, the last time they checked, was a serious crime worthy of a firing squad in the United States. They drilled it into her that if any of those happened, she should rip off her clothes, bruise herself a little, and then run out to the street and have someone call the law immediately on her husband.

Rose winced. She pretended to be indignant about that last piece of advice, telling her enablers that in all the years her parents had been together, her mom had never called the police on her father.

"All I can say to that is you are becoming self-righteous in this land of individual rights and the pursuit of happiness. What is wrong with you, kid?" Doris Kamalu asked in annoyance.

"Nothing is wrong with me," Rose said.

"All right then. Let us compare apples to apples, okay? In the male-dominated society we all came from, divorce was never an option for your parents. That held the same for your grandparents and your great-grandparents on both sides of your family. They stayed together till death did them part. I am not saying it is wrong, but you plan to leave your husband for another man, right? So why do you draw the line at calling the cops on him? What a double standard! Be careful. Otherwise your self-righteousness will be your undoing. Mark my words," Doris said.

Rose replied that it would be wrong for her to deviate from the good example her mom had set.

"You all know this. Back home, we do not call the police to arrest family members, no matter what they do to us. No, when we have situations and dramas in our families even in our big cities, we bring in family elders to mediate. No one ever invites the police or other outsiders to examine the family's dirty laundry."

"That is a function of a society assigning more rights to the community than it does to individuals," Doris said. "And that is wrong as you will soon find out. The good news is that America has rectified that wrong by giving more rights to the states than it does to the central government. Anyone can call the police on anyone. It's nothing personal. So please do not drag us back to the dark days when individual rights were subjugated to those of the rulers. Your husband represents the ruling elite, and we are here to overthrow that."

Rose said that no matter how permissive and accommodating America had been to them, it would be wrong for them to act as if they were Americans by birth. She said they should know better than to stomp on their African heritage. All her counselors were offended at her insolence, none more so than Doris. She was slightly older and claimed to be wealthier than the rest of the gang. She took a closer look at Rose and noticed changes in her the others had missed. Doris couldn't hide her disdain.

"Do you think that your mother will be okay with you living with your husband and yet doing another man to the extent of carrying his baby?"

"Doris, please," Evelyn Ukwa said, admonishing Doris for her blunt talk.

"I am sorry, ladies, for getting a little bit carried away, but this does not look good. We are sticking our necks out to help this child sidestep the mine fields that no one knew enough about, or cared enough to warn us about, after we were conned and brought over to America to be beasts of burden to conscienceless men who wanted us to take care of them so they would not have to live in nursing homes when old age arrived. You ladies know that this association is trying to help liberate this child, and we are doing it free of charge.

"I am an excellent judge of character, and I can tell you right off the bat that we are dealing with an ingrate here. Listen to her closely. We ask nothing of her, but she is being childish and churlish as if we need something from her. She must realize that we are all well-established, independent ladies. We have money in the bank and it is in dollars. This girl has nothing that we need."

"Aunty Doris, please. I know that you are upset, but do not break our law of decorum. We are all sisters," Evelyn pleaded again. "This child needs us. She may not realize it because she is like a chicken placed in a confined space. Her feet have been tied together for too long. Her oxygen is low, affecting the functioning of her brain. Even after she has been freed, she still thinks she is still in bondage. We need to liberate her mind gently with grace and with compassion. Please go easy on her. Work on her mind first. Do not tell her only what this association opposes. Tell her about the good things we do. Tell her what we stand for and what we do every day for young African women in this country."

"Still, she needs to know that we are doing her a big favor," Doris said. "She needs to start showing appreciation, if not respect. She can't do a thing for me. As William Shakespeare correctly said, 'I hate ingratitude in a girl more than I hate an empty glass of German ale.'"

That was a misquotation of the Bard, but the other women applauded.

"As I said, please let us not give up on her," Evelyn said.

"I am a loving, compassionate woman of God," Doris said, "but I am not going to let her insult me and get away with it, because doing so would unconsciously induce me to shut the door of compassion on more needful young girls looking for me to rescue them from slaverys. You all know I want to see young women freed from the control of fabulously rich but illiterate African men. That is my passion. I do these rescue operations despite being very busy. Therefore, it's an enormous insult to me for some kid to imply that I need anything from her. As you all know, I am the director of nursing at my job.

"With my nurse practitioner degree in advanced neuroscience, I make more money than medical doctors. I live in an exclusive area on Green Pasture Land. My house is on a ten-acre spread. My property has its own lake. Because I have been sumptuously blessed, without fanfare and without seeking praise, I use my blessings in the cause of freedom for young women who have been worse than trafficked. They have been unequally yoked with my arch-enemies, pot-bellied, bald-headed African men."

"Aunty Doris, as sister Evelyn asked you earlier, tell her about the specific good things we do for our gender," Eno Ette said. "As you know, there's an Ibibio tribal adage that says that if you pull a louse or a leach from the back of a dog without showing it to the dog, the dog might conclude that you are pinching it or damaging its fur. It will attack you. But if you show the pests to the dog, the dog will be grateful and think of you as a liberator and its best friend. So show this child that we are making life better for young African girls."

"Okay," Doris said. "A few years ago, a very beautiful girl living in a cramped apartment in this city fell out of love with her husband. She found another man, who promised to treat her like a queen. She was nice enough to tell the no-good husband she was moving on with her life. She filed for divorce. He did not fight it, and her petition was granted. She bought a huge house and moved in. Soon after, a large quantity of narcotics she oversaw at the hospital where she worked came up missing. Was that a coincidence? I think not! She was arrested and locked up. Charges were brought against her. She soon lost custody of her children. Her ex-husband withdrew the petition he had filed to change her status to permanent resident. She got deported before we knew about it.

"Vivian got wind of the story and brought it to my attention. This association took action. We sent some of our members to Nigeria to see if there was a spiritual dimension to the situation. We also hired the best team of immigration lawyers in town. To make a long story short, we brought this woman back to be with her kids. She's become a citizen of this country, thanks to this group. Our organization is needed. Yes, it may not be needed by the likes of Rose. But if she looks around she will notice there is not even one chapter of the African Students Union left in America or Europe. That's because all the African enclaves that agitated for independence in the last century got it, so that union no longer had what the French call a *raison d'etre*. The organization was no longer needed.

"The evidence is there for all to see. Every leader of that group has retreated to his secure corner, reaping the fruits of his labor. Closer to home, tribalism will not let the Nigerian Unity Association in the United States get off the ground. The Nigerians who wanted to change their country by coming to America to attend universities in the 1970s and '80s have either died out or returned home to become senators, or government functionaries. No one hears of the NUA anymore.

"On the other hand, our group will always be here so long as young girls are conned to come to America to become the property of pot-bellied African men whose fathers did not have a college education but who had more money than some national governments do. This child does not know it, but she needs us."

"I know she does not know it, but please forgive her," Caroline Thomas said. "We are all she has got in this land where there are fewer African women of valor than there are African men trying to keep African women in bondage. Let us try to be ladies, please. We all know that the men who forced us to come to America are not treating us like ladies. They would love nothing more than to see us fight each other. No, I take that back. They would also love to see state troopers flashing blue-and-red lights behind us in our SUVs, slapping cuffs on us, and taking us to downtown. Let us not put more arrows into their quivers by making it look like we are perpetually at war with ourselves, because we are not."

"Okay. Here is a question for Rose," Doris said, returning to her leadership role. "Did your dad ever take undue advantage of your mom?"

"No, he never did," Rose answered.

"Well, here is a news flash for you. The man who brought you to America had a plan to buy a $250,000 house on the outskirts of the city. For that plan to come to fruition, he needed to commandeer an inexperienced girl from home. So by paying your way to this country, he actually took advantage of you, because he did not bring you here for your good but for himself and for his good."

"He did?" Rose asked.

"Of course he did. Where have you been? It's a scam. It's happening all over Nigeria," Doris said.

"I am sorry for not getting it."

"That is okay, dear. To the battle-tested like us, it is a simple logic, but to the mathematically challenged like you, it is a revelation. Not everyone can figure it out. That is the reason I am taking valuable time from my highly profitable business to carefully explain to you the theory behind your importation to America. We want to make the facts work for you as they have worked for us."

"I appreciate all that you do for me, aunties," Rose said.

"That mangy dog that brought you to America did an unspeakably evil thing to you," Doris said. "Ravening wolf that he is, he took advantage of you when you were most vulnerable. He knew that you were young and beautiful and that like lots of young and beautiful African girls tired of farm work, you were desperate to come to America. He also knew you would do anything to realize that dream. Trying to escape poverty on the farm, you were incapable of rational thought. He could sense that and used psychology on you. He waved his ill-gotten dollars. He sent subliminal messages to your brain, and you mindlessly responded to all of them. He blinded you with hard currency to lure you into exclusive hotels where even janitors are dressed in tuxedos. All these places were in the crazy, fast, and immoral city of Lagos, where you knew nobody but him. You were forced to depend on him.

"He seized and abused that opportunity. He primed you, an innocent, Sunday-school-attending little girl who, prior to meeting him, had never had any drink stronger than Pepsi-Cola. He messed up your mind with adult beverages. That is when he took advantage of you. But now you are in America. Here, everyone is business-oriented. A business is not a passive entity. It has assets. It has liabilities. Therefore, this man must be made to pay for taking advantage of you, an innocent, vulnerable girl. There is no statute of limitation on collecting what he owes you. He has to pay. I hate him already. I hate him at least as much as I hated my ex after I found out that he had dated a senior-year roommate of mine when I was a flat-chested teenager in my freshman year. That man returned the next year and went out with another of my roommates after the other one graduated.

"He returned in my third year to go out with yet another roommate of mine. I suspect he must have had his radar trained on me, because after I left my training bras behind, he noticed me and began his enticements. He set perfect traps for me, and I fell headlong into all of them. First, without even knowing my name, not to mention having me fitted for them, he brought me assorted panties and designer-size 34-DDD bras without wires, my favorites, from America. To the envy and surprise of my roommates and other girls who saw me try them on, they fit like they were tailor-made for me. Those things looked so good on me I felt they were the only clothing items I needed on or off campus.

Most of the lecturers who made their money selling hard-to-find textbooks to students, noticed my new upper body and gave me lecture-notes free of charge. I even received gifts from professors. Some of them gave me A-pluses for courses I did not take and would have flunked if I did. Those bras put me in a class all by myself. I suddenly became the envy of all the high-maintenance girls on campus. They wondered which politician was my sugar daddy and wanted to hang around me, because they thought my man had more of a taste for the good life than theirs. That man, with no input from me, made me the center of the universe for those well-to-do girls. I have no sympathy for him. And I have no sympathy for your facilitator either. You and I are playthings to these men. You deserve your pound of flesh from his hide just like I got mine. Do not hesitate to take it. It is rightly yours."

The other women chimed in to support Doris's position about what Rose was owed. They warned Rose that humility was not a virtue in America. She tried to clear up a point one of them had made, but they were impatient with the interruption. They accused her of being a wet blanket and derided her for showing weakness when resolve was called for. They told Rose that was the mistake a lot of layaway wives made in America. They warned her and other newly minted layaway wives against living in America as if they still lived in Africa.

The women begged Rose to snap out of what they called the African mentality. They said that mentality was responsible for preventing African women from reaching their potential in America. They told her the benefits of living in America with an American mentality.

Rose said she did not want to find herself on the wrong side of the law, get thrown in jail, and be deported back to Africa and poverty. The women asked if she knew enough US history to identify who had said that in America, there is nothing to fear but fear itself. She shook her head. They assured Rose that the state of Texas was a woman's best friend, because when police were called to deal with a domestic situation, they usually asked the man to leave his domicile and to go somewhere to cool off. And if police kept getting called to the same address, they would issue a restraining order requiring the man to stay at least hundred yards from the house and the female occupant. That way the woman's safety was never threatened.

Rose could not believe that a pro-women law like that existed anywhere outside of heaven. The women told her that most modern American laws were written after women were given the vote. They said the right to vote not only gave women control of their lives but showed men-folks that their female counter-parts were no longer to be treated like pork bellies at auctions. They told her that studies showed that when women took complete control of their lives the world would win a victory. That would be so because women are not just the so-called fair sex but are fair in most of their dealings. They told her that women would be responsible for finding the cures for all forms of cancer, even prostate cancer. They assured Rose that if her husband lashed out at her, his US wealth would be legally transferred to her.

As Rose tried to wrap her mind around all the civic and legal information being dumped on her, her enablers noticed the confusion on her face. They were happy for her. They interpreted her facial expression to mean she was already rich but did not know it. They assured her that all she needed to do was subtly push Emmanuel to act foolishly around her and then call the police immediately. They promised her that after she got the police involved and her aggressor removed from the house, the case would no longer be between her and Emmanuel but between him and Texas. They told her that at their own expense, they would hire a divorce attorney who had proven clout with family-court judges. The aggressive lawyer would not only remove her from the abusive relationship, they said, but would persuade the court to grant her at least 75 percent of her husband's possessions, which they referred to as community property, as allowed under the state's marriage laws. The women also told Rose that it was time for her to quit her second job.

"No, I can't stop working a second job," she said. "I am even looking for a third one. I have to send money home to my parents to pay for my younger brothers' and sisters' school fees."

"Well, it is indeed twisted logic, but the truth is that you will get more rewards from this system by working less," Caroline said.

"How does that work?" Rose asked.

"Well, seeing how you do not have children with this imbecile yet, and this being Texas, it will be an uphill task to convince even the most liberal family-court judge to slap your husband with alimony and child-support payments. But you are entitled to get his property through another route called common law. However, there is a caveat. This route will work best for you if your tax returns for the previous year show that you made less money than your husband did in that year. In this state when community property is on the cutting board, the lower-earning spouse usually gets the giant share. Work less to make more. That is the formula," Caroline said.

"That is mathematically impossible," Rose argued.

"Where we all came from? Yes. But here in the land of the free, the unequivocal answer is no," Doris said. "There is an important principle at work here. Given that you just got here, no one expects you to know this, but make it work for you. I'm not a tax attorney, but I know this for a fact: the Internal Revenue Service gives you money back if you did not earn a decent living in the previous year. The same principle automatically applies in when a marriage comes apart. So stop arguing with us. This is America.

"We have been through a lot in our young lives with the men who brought us to this country to make themselves rich. If life were fair to the point where women were presidents of most colleges, we would all be given at least two honorary degrees apiece for our sufferings. What we are saying with all humility is that though we did not get university degrees in Nigeria as you did, we know America better than you do. So let our collective-experience show you how to make this country work for you. We offer you words of wisdom. A wise girl heeds them and becomes wiser and rich. We supposed that you are a wise girl. That is the reason we are banding together to free you from your husband's bondage.

"More important, despite your resistance, we are building the foundation to make you rich in a short time. We are a sisterhood. More than that, like you have been told, we are a regime. We make things happen. We've got each other's backs. Trust us. By way of further assurance, we are not doing this so we can ask for a consultation fee after your ship comes in. Again, we are a sisterhood. We have all been wronged by dads who dominated and oppressed our moms, by wicked men who continue to see us, the descendants of voiceless women, as cash cows, pleasure centers, and baby machines. Our only interest is to make sure that every one of our boats rises when the tide comes in."

CHAPTER 10

Before Rose was admitted to a university in her country, her natural endowments landed her a job teaching high school English Literature. She did not like the job. It appeared that the job did not like her either, because she could tell that the students, who were only a little younger than she was, could sense she was not up to snuff on the subject she was assigned to teach them. They made her nervous and mistake-prone. But before she sought to lessen her stress level by quitting that job, she had become an item with another young person working as a third-class clerk in the principal's office. His name was Dennis Mbabar, and he could not wait to leave Nigeria. Before long, they were talking marriage and how to get to America at other people's expense. He coached her on how to spot and to ingratiate herself with the Nigerian men who had lived abroad too long. Such Nigerians, Dennis informed his lover, briefly returned home to search for, fall in love with, and marry virgins, whom they would take back to America within the span of 30 days.

That was the man who, according to Mary, had been calling Rose at work. But after Rose received a verbal warning from her supervisor about the personal calls she had been taking on company time, she gave her lover the number to the phone in the break room. Her lover usually called during lunch.

Mary had told Emmanuel about this. She also helped him to install an electronic bugging device on the pay phone to record the conversations between Rose and the lunch-time caller. Mary was an expert at making communication devices do things they were not designed to do. She messed with the break-room phone and programmed it to send a call from a particular number in California to a recording device that Rose's husband had set up in the attic of his house. In a short time, he had recorded hours and hours of phone conversations between his wife and the lover. Rose's husband could not wait to get home from his job. The highlight of his day was to reach home ahead of his wife and to listen to the day's recording before she returned. From one of those recordings he learned that it was just a stroke of luck that caused Rose to live with him longer than the first week after her arrival in America.

The plan that Rose and her paramour had hatched back in Nigeria was for her to get to the United States first and then to find a way to bring him over on a visitor's visa. But once Rose departed Nigeria, Dennis Mbabar made other plans that did not include her. He found a much younger woman and decided to stay in Nigeria to comfort her for as long as she needed him. He left Rose in the dark while she was doing all she could to get him over as they had agreed.

Rose's husband also learned from the recordings that when Dennis finally came to the States, despite Rose's pleadings, he went to live in California. Rose had begged him to move to Texas, Alabama, or another state close enough that she could visit him on her off days. But he told her it could be unhealthy for him to be so near her husband on a long-term basis and in Texas, where every adult male was entitled to carry at least two guns in his pickup truck and had the state's backing to use them when threatened and to ask questions later. This standard applied particularly in the settlement of issues concerning the loss of affection.

Rose had pleaded with him not to exaggerate the risk involved, adding that she was worth whatever risk was entailed. But after he cited and also sent her a newspaper clip concerning the recent case of a young Nigerian male who was shot and killed by an older Nigerian-born college professor for what the police called loss of affection, she agreed that if a Nigerian who did not grow up in a household with guns could in America take out his wife's lover and serve no jail time for the homicide, maybe it was not a such a great idea for her lover to move so close to her. Therefore, at intervals, she would rent a room at the Bounty Harvest Hill Hotel for him to visit so they could strengthen the bond between them.

CHAPTER 11

Ekaete "Kate" Ikor, a fiery member of Rose's support group, intended to have lunch with Silver Briggs, but as she was waiting, she spied Rose in the restaurant. Rose was looking very pale and sitting alone at the cafeteria table where they always met. Not wanting to jump to conclusions, she approached Rose to ask a personal question. Though it was not a big deal in America, this was something people in Africa did not usually do.

"Are you expecting, Sister Rose?" Kate asked.

"Yes, I am. Is it that obvious? Am I already showing?"

"That means you have been consorting with that slaver after we, your family, clearly told you to find ways not to let that happen. Did he force himself on you, and if so, why didn't you report the assault to the regime or to the police as we had urged you to do?"

"No. That is not how and what happened."

"I have seen what happened. So bring me up to speed on the when and the where."

"Well …"

"How can we help you if you are unwilling to help us help you? This is not good!"

"What I am trying to say is that my husband did not cause this pregnancy."

"What?"

"That's right. This bundle of joy is not my husband's."

"No? Then this is more sadness than joy. Wouldn't you agree?"

"No, madam," Rose replied.

"That is such a comfort," Kate said, raising her voice a couple of notches. At that point, Eno Ette walked in.

"I am very sorry, madam, to disappoint all of you," Rose said.

"Please stop this nonsense. At this juncture, I think a full explanation rather than a mea culpa would be in order, because we had also said no pregnancy until you were safely out of your husband's house."

"This bundle of joy belongs to my lover. He lives in California. I used to go with him long before my sponsor married me and brought me to America."

"In a way, it is commendable that the pregnancy is not your husband's. But that creates its own set of obstacles."

"What do you mean by that? You said I should not have relations with my husband. But you did not say anything about making babies with another man, did you?"

"Yes, we did."

"No, I swear you did not, madam. I do not recall you telling …"

"At least we implied it."

"I am sorry, madam, but that does not work for me. I am like an assembly-line mechanic. I work only at my station and only with the parts I'm supplied. No extra duties."

"Then how did you gain admission to the government-run University of Nigeria? Okay, I get it. You must be one of those extra-beautiful girls who do not bother to take the foolish entrance exams the rest of us are required to take, right?"

"Yes, madam, you are right. You know how the system works over there, right? I did not create it. I simply made it work for me. That's all beautiful girls have to do."

"That is my country. Our former national anthem says, 'Nigeria, we held thee, our own dear native land.' Beauty and/or family connections are guaranteed to propel good-looking girls to the top all the time ahead of others who are better qualified. What a country!"

"As I said, I did not create that system. You were once young and very beautiful yourself. Don't you remember how men with money and power used to fall over each other to make you their mistress? That has not changed. It won't change," Rose said.

"Do not get me wrong, dear. I am not blaming you. Nature does not permit a vacuum to exist. Therefore, in a nation of blind folks, those who see just a little are destined and duty-bound to become kings. But we are in America, where people of integrity won't allow greed to over-rule justice and fairness. Did you tell your standby lover that you are carrying his baby while married to another man? If so, what did he say?"

"I like the way you put that, madam. That is so apt. 'Standby lover' as in the standby power generators we crank up back home when our regular electric supply is inadequate or unavailable. Yes, I have informed my standby lover of this bundle of joy. Got any more questions?"

"No, sister, and you do not have to be sassy with me, okay? You do not know it now, but you have created more problems than you started out with. More sadness than joy lies ahead of you. What are your plans now?"

"I am planning to move to California."

"And when would that be?"

"He told me that would not be a good idea at this time, given that he does not have his own place yet and is squatting with friends. So I am going to hold off moving to California until he is ready for us."

"That means your husband will continue caring not just for you but for another man's baby. Even Lucifer will find something wrong with that situation."

"I guess so."

"How long do you plan to drag your husband through this raw deal?"

"I do not know how long it will be before we move to California. With the eternal drought parching California right now, nothing is certain. He told me that it is harder to find accommodations in the City of Angels than in the Big Apple, and more expensive too."

"That is just a cop-out. Do you hear me?"

"No, it is not. I know he is trustworthy."

"He is a pig—to you, a trustworthy pig; to us, a regular pig. And just like any self-respecting boar, he could not miss the mating call of a desperate sow in heat. But now that nurturing is called for, your Napoleon is nowhere to be found. All of a sudden, his pen is too small to accommodate his sow. In practical terms, my friend, you're no longer his equal. You are his partner no more. From now on, you will have to fill out a guest form and clear security to see him. You do not award a man like that a certificate of trustworthiness. He has not earned it."

"My guy is different. He is a very giving and caring man."

"I do not want to rain on your parade, dear. You have not completely leveled with us, but based on the little information you have thus far supplied, the man is an opportunist just like George Orwell's Napoleon. He is as exploitative as the men who run your country. All of them are cut from the same cloth. They are all out for themselves. They should not be trusted despite their gift of gab. So, for the sake of my sanity, please stop heaping encomiums on the man who has hung this bundle of sadness on you. Right now, if he is the least bit excited at the thought of you, it is because someone else is paying for the cow and providing pasture for her while he is getting the milk free. He has created a hell for you while he enjoys himself, and you do not even know it. He has you seriously snowed. He is no good."

"I know for fact that you are wrong, and after you have met him, you will completely agree with me," Rose said.

"I am sorry, but our sisterhood has no intention of breaking bread with any man whose goal is to keep one of our members barefoot and pregnant," Silver said as she joined them.

"My Californian does not fall into that category of men. In the time I have known him, he has shown that he wants what is best for me. He will do no less now that I am carrying his baby. He is an entirely good man, always looking out for me. My move to this country was his idea. Left to my own devices, I would still be in Nigeria trying to fight other beautiful girls on my way up the civil service ladder by using my body. The man loves me. I just know it. I cannot explain it to you."

"Then why wouldn't he risk everything to be united with his woman and his child when they need him most? Did you say that he used to be a seminarian? Then he should know that love is all about giving and not about receiving and taking advantage of others. As one of the early followers of The Way, The Truth, The Light said about the Master, he loved his church so much that he gave his life for it. Why won't your lover sacrifice his comfort for your safety?"

"There is no doubt in my mind that he will send for us as soon as he is able to find housing. That is what he told me, and I have no reason to doubt him."

"Fine," Silver said, "but the longer it takes him to transform those words into action, the more legal obstacles are thrown in your way, not by your despicable husband and his nosy friends, all known enemies of your advancement in this country, but by the system, the state of Texas. This state has a vested interest in the way its most vulnerable citizens—children and the elderly—are treated by the rest of us with sound knees, twenty-twenty vision, and good risk-management skills. The system is suspicious of able-bodied people like you. Therefore, if you give birth to this baby while you are still living under the same roof as your husband, the child's birth certificate will carry your husband's name, not your lover's. That is how the state protects its young and vulnerable. So to avoid a drawn-out fight with the system, you better tell your Californian that his chickens have come home to roost and that he must get on the ball right away. By the way, have you told your husband yet that while you are in his house, you are expecting another man's baby?"

"No, I have not and I do not intend to."

"Good, but how long do you plan on keeping it that way? Something has to give at some point. You know that men are a cunning bunch. During the hunting and gathering era in this planet's past, men used to sneak up on huge animals such as mammoths and did them in. These days, they are not above sneaking up on us, the so-called weaker sex. Do you see where I am going with this?"

"No, I am not quite there yet. A tutorial would be in order."

"Well, your husband went to college here in the land of the sneaky CIA and FBI. He is not totally dumb, so along the way he must have learned something. You know that a pregnancy is not one of those things that can be kept hidden from the public forever. Besides, the long, hot summer will soon be upon us. You will not be wearing heavy winter clothes as you are now. If you are dressed in winter clothes even on a mild summer day, men may not notice the contrast, but other women will, and they will consider it their duty to inform your husband that something is up. Your cover will surely be blown in a few weeks. A pregnancy is like a seed sitting in soil in a flower pot. With time, it will start showing and will outgrow its confinement. Are you going to wait till then to tell your husband? Most men do not appreciate finding out about their wives' pregnancies in the fortieth week or while the wives are being wheeled from labor to the delivery room. Your husband may be one of those men with whom such surprises do not sit well."

"Will telling him be a good thing for me or not?"

"I do not know. What I do know is that men are sneaky—African men more so, because forgiveness is an alien concept to them. Tit for tat is a huge part of their religion of self-worship. That, plus controlling us the way their daddies controlled their mommies, is what they live for."

Rose had failed to disclose one bit of information to her support group. She had forgotten to mention that since she had told her lover how far along her pregnancy was, he had not called her back—not during lunch or any other time, as he used to before she gave him the good news. She had also forgotten to mention that she had no way of getting in touch with her lover, because she did not have his number. It appeared that he always called her from a pay phone. So, at a time when she needed to be in contact with him on a regular basis, not just so she could update him on the legal implications of her sojourn in Texas with her husband, but also to feel closer to him, she had no way of reaching him. The women assumed Rose was in constant contact with her lover, and since she did not see any benefit in trying to correct the assumption, she let sleeping dogs lie.

CHAPTER 12

ON A HOT and humid day, Mary called Emmanuel, saying she had a disturbing piece of information for him and asking him to see her right away. Hearing the urgency in her voice, he assumed she wanted to borrow money. He found a good excuse not to meet with her, saying he could not make it because he was working overtime. Mary would not take no for an answer and kept pushing for a meeting. Exasperated, Emmanuel agreed to meet with her after church at a laundry shop she often used.

When Emmanuel arrived at the Love Laundromat, Mary was waiting outside. She had already washed, dried, folded, and bagged her laundry. She invited Emmanuel to come inside the place. The traffic was not as heavy as usual, but the place was noisy since the few customers in there were washing down comforters in the big washing machines. The atmosphere conspired against Emmanuel and Mary. Though they sat next to each other, they could not hear one another, and that was not entirely due to their differing accents. Mary suggested they sit in his car if the air conditioning was working. Emmanuel said they should have brunch at Las Cubanas Caribanas, a nearby Spanish restaurant. Mary thought that was a good idea and agreed.

She gave him a hand loading the laundry into his car and they drove off.

****

The moving company arrived at a little after seven in the morning. Rose had instructed the movers to delay their arrival until her husband had departed the house for his teaching job. But Emmanuel had fooled Rose. He had driven only a short distance and parked his car nearby, giving Rose the impression that he had left for the high school. From his vantage point, Emmanuel saw the moving truck pull up to his town house. He waited. Per Rose's instruction, the movers worked frantically to load the truck. After Emmanuel observed that the truck was almost full, he drove up and blocked it with his vehicle. He entered the house without speaking to the movers, pulled up a bar stool, and sat down in the middle of the living room under a ceiling fan. Rose was upstairs taping boxes. After a while, she came downstairs to ask the movers if they needed something to drink and to tell them the boxes upstairs were ready to go into the truck. She was startled to see Emmanuel.

"What are you doing home so early?" she asked her husband.

"The last time I checked—this morning, as a matter of fact—I lived at this address. More important, I am not just paying for this house, but it is listed under my name at the title office. Got any more questions?" Emmanuel asked.

"Should you not be teaching school at this hour? You are supposed to be at work. Why are you not? What happened?"

"Though they were nothing more than property and other people's investments, even slaves used to be given days off when they hurt, if not for good behavior. As your indentured servant, am I not allowed to come in from the rain once in a while so I won't die and cost you your investment?" Emmanuel asked.

He jumped down from the bar stool, went to the entertainment center, and put a tape in the cassette player. At that moment, one of the movers noticed an unusual bulge on Emmanuel, which caused his shorts to sag. In a panicky voice, the worker told the foreman that Emmanuel was "packing heat" and that it looked like a multiple murder-suicide was in the offing. The foreman questioned Rose, and she confirmed that she had not told Emmanuel she was moving out. All the movers raced for the door.

Emmanuel locked the door behind them and turned up the volume on the amplifier. Rose heard her own voice, distinct and clear, coming from the speakers. She also heard another voice. It was Dennis Mbabar's. The recording seemed to have been made at a professional studio. Rose began to sweat even though the air conditioner was cranked up all the way. She felt like she was losing her mind. For about half an hour, she stood dumbfounded. There was no mistaking that these were the intimate conversations she had with the Californian. But who had recorded them? That was the question she needed to answer. She began to cry. The more she heard, the more she cried. Rose knew for a fact that her husband was not standing knee-deep in dollars as the people at home perceived him to be. So how did he get her lover to betray her like this, recording their every intimate moments together?

Just as that thought entered her mind, Emmanuel inserted another tape into a boom box. At the same time, he unfurled a projection screen on the wall above the entertainment center. The presentation began with real time superimposed on the top of the screen and with Rose arriving at her main job. The next clip showed her exiting the parking garage. The next showed her parking her car at the back of the Harvest Hill Hotel and getting into an elevator. The clip that followed showed the time and the date on the nightstand in the hotel room Rose had entered. It showed her getting out of her scrubs and throwing them on the floor beside the bed.

As Rose got into the bed, the screen panned back to her job and showed her supervisor demanding to know her whereabouts.

Emmanuel pulled out a weapon from his pocket and equipped it with silencer.

Rose sank to her knees and begged for her life. Emmanuel placed another tape in another boom box. On that one Rose was assuring her lover that she was neither in love with her husband nor sleeping with him on a regular basis. As evidence, she pointed out that not only had she convinced her husband that he was the reason she could not become pregnant, but she had sent him on a wild goose chase, spending time and money to fix nonexistent urological problems.

Since Emmanuel had blocked the moving company truck with his car, two of the younger movers stealthily entered the carport to retrieve a floor jack they had seen lying there. They needed it to jack up the front end of Emmanuel's car to push it out of their way so they could leave.

Through the living room window, one of the movers spied Emmanuel holding a gun to the head of a kneeling Rose. He ran back to the truck and informed his boss that a murder was about to take place. The boss, whose name was David Green, tiptoed to the house. He inserted a pin in the lock and pushed the door open. It was Emmanuel's turn to be startled. He was so surprised by the sudden intrusion into his private business that the heavy Colt .45 he was holding to his wife's head slipped from his hand as David put him in a choke hold. Though Emmanuel recovered the gun, he was baffled. How did the foreman get into the house? Was he one of those witches who claimed to have the ability to walk through locked doors and walls at will? That was supposed to take place in Africa only! No, the man was an American, not an African. He could not have been a witch. Emmanuel's brain could not process what had happened. He knew he had locked the door, but he could not recall if he had activated the dead bolt.

Emmanuel had no way of knowing that David had been a professional burglar and an expert lock-pick, who prided himself on being able to open even the toughest locks in seconds. But the police had eventually nabbed him.

David was a man of few words. In prison, he kept to himself. Older prisoners respected his wish to be left alone. Young folks, on the other hand, who had been informed by their trusty friends of David's skills, wanted to learn some pointers from him. When he was not forthcoming, they said he was acting like he was better than the other inmates. He told the older inmates that he did not come to prison to learn how to be what he called a "bad-ass criminal" since he already was one and more. He said his lack of interest in learning new crime skills was the reason he did not hang around the day room. David said he was an accomplished pickpocket and con man who had nothing to prove to rookie criminals and law enforcement.

At intake—when people reporting to prison are assessed for their "free world" skills, assigned chores, counseled, and made to swap their street clothes for prison uniforms— David had admitted that his crimes supported a heroin habit, so he was assigned to a drug-addiction intervention program called Hi-way to Real Freedom. Having entered that program and been a model prisoner, he received parole. He remained tethered to the system through the parole board, which retained the right to resentence him to a hasher prison stint if he re-offended. Since David was taking all kinds of prescribed and over-the-counter medications to deal with various medical problems, particularly an overactive prostrate, he was determined to stay out of prison. He bought a used bobtail truck, hired fellow parolees, and started a moving company in his wife's name.

Now David stood between Emmanuel and his wife.

"Get out of my way before this thing goes off," Emmanuel demanded, pointing the gun inter-changeably at David and Rose.

"That is so funny that you said that," David said.

"What is so funny? Do you know that this thing is loaded and can go off anytime?"

"I am not sure if back in your tribal land, your machetes can cut down even soft woods like banana trees on their own."

"What do you mean?"

"Machetes are not known to work all by themselves. Neither are guns."

"Who had said otherwise?"

"You did."

"Excuse me, sir. Please do not put words in my mouth. I am a college-educated man. I was born and raised in a farming community. I would not say such a thing."

"You implied it."

"I did not."

"Well regardless, I have read that after the initial and the primary human residents of the Garden of Eden violated the terms of their occupancy permit and, a flaming scimitar that could turn every way a potential enemy turned was stationed near the Tree of Life to keep the couple from further violation of their rental agreement."

"What is your point?" Emmanuel asked.

"Unlike that flaming sword, which I think was solar-powered and one of a kind, the tool in your hand cannot do damage all by itself. When firearms do damage, it is usually at the behest of their human handlers. But by ordering me to get out of your way before the weapon in your hand goes off, you are implying that guns, machetes, and other weapons can operate independent of their human enablers. Let me ask you this. Are you one of those people unwilling to take responsibility when their weapons cause harm?"

"You have lost me. What are you talking about?"

"My guys said your wife told them you are a cab driver."

"Yes. I teach school and work other jobs, but also drive a taxi, and I am not apologizing for that. It is a job, period. There are lots of Africans in this country with master's degrees and even PhDs in the glove compartments of the cabs they drive. They can't get jobs in their fields because of their accents. Just as you are in the moving business, they drive cabs so they can keep pursuing the American dream. They are in hot pursuit of happiness. They do what they have to do to take care of their families. No apologies for working."

"Please understand I am not putting down any job that puts food on the table. Jobs are the cure for poverty. That has been settled. The point I am trying to make is that, as a highly educated individual, you should know that the moment you squeeze the part called a trigger on that thing in your hand, your wife will die from a projectile that thing sends out into her."

"Hello, that was the main idea until you decided to take a bullet for her. Thanks for volunteering. Now I am going to kill you, her, and any eyewitness as well."

"What?"

"That's right. You are facing this firing squad freely and willingly," Emmanuel said.

"I am sure you know that taking a human life is a very serious matter in these parts. And you are contemplating on taking at least two, right?"

"The answer is an emphatic yes."

"In that case, before you do this, let us hear your best-thought-out excuse for making motherless kids out of your babies, who at this moment are sleeping innocently upstairs. As for myself, I do not care. In my case, death is considered a job hazard. My long-suffering wife would finally get rewarded with a big payday for her devotion to me all these years. My life insurance would pay her eighty-eight thousand dollars after Uncle Sam had taken out taxes on my estate. So you will be doing me a big favor."

The two men stood eyeballing each other.

"Your best argument for what you are about to do, please, sir. We do not have all day," David said.

Emmanuel suddenly burst into tears.

"This woman is the most heartless of all the lying, conniving, devilish women on earth. For causing me to be poor and destitute, she deserves to die a horrible death and to have her corpse desecrated. I will ensure that."

"That is bold of you, but I thought only judges and courts are authorized to make life-and-death decisions in these United States," David said.

"That is true. I understand that vengeance is not mine. However, after you have been mercilessly wronged, inhumanly used, and your resources stolen as mine have been, nature sides with you when you choose to right the wrong. The world benefits from a reduction in the number of those who cause the righteous to fall. You could say that the death sentence I am about to carry out on this devil is a selfless act of righteousness on behalf of humanity. It is for a greater good."

"You brand a homicide a greater good for humanity, eh? That is the same argument I have been using on my wife. I have not been able to convince her that my drug use is my contribution to the world's agricultural growth. You need to help me talk to my wife after this."

"Your thesis is not valid, but mine is."

"That's not fair."

"A lot of good and wholesome things will wash over the earth after the deviance and the progression of evil has been stopped."

"Do not let my wife hear you say that. To her, that would be like saying you kill for love. She would say that your statement is invalid because it has contradictory components. I am not religious, but have you ever considered why all the major religions of the world, even the nontheistic ones, consider forgiveness a virtue?"

"Crimes against humanity should not be mentioned in the same breath with forgiveness. So please do not do that. Evil does not know how to stop itself. It is not equipped to do that. It has to be stopped. Otherwise it muddies up heaven's plan for mankind to be moved to the next level, to a place of long-term happiness and rest for those whose good deeds are more numerous than their bad deeds."

"As I said, I am not a very religious guy, but my wife, who teaches Sunday School Bible classes, says that when we humans set out to help God run his world without consulting him first, we usually end up messing up his perfect plan. She cites the case of the patriarch Abraham and his wife Sarah. With good intentions, the couple tried to help God speed up things in their lives and ended up creating a mess. So set aside vengeance. You do not need to speed up your wife's day of judgment. It will come of its own accord and sweet time.

"It could be that like many Africans in America, you have done well for yourself, as your houses inside gated communities can testify. You contribute a lot of money to charity. You have met all standards of righteousness and therefore feel that forgiveness is not an option. But as an observer of the human condition and as someone who has often been on the receiving end of forgiveness, I know that it heals both the giver and the receiver. You will greatly benefit from doing the right thing, forgiving."

"Thanks, but no thanks," Emmanuel said. "As you can see, I do not live in a gated community. This woman has seen to that. Keep that forgiveness and offer it to those who truly need it. As for me, I am destroyed, and my credit is too. I am in bankruptcy."

"I may be wrong about this, but you cannot fault others for handling your money the wrong way, as if it belonged to the military government of a Third-World nation."

"The truth is that without taking out enormous student loans while in graduate school, I would not have been able to finance this woman's trip to this country. I owe more on student loans than those who studied medicine and I am not making a six-figure salary even with three jobs."

"I am sorry to hear that, but killing her won't lessen your debt load. The loan will still have to be paid. In the United States, filing for chapter 11 does not wipe out indebtedness to the student loan program. If you kill your wife and yourself, Uncle Sam will still come after your estate. He's good at that."

"This woman is evil. She made me bite off more than I could chew. Instead of helping me escape the financial abyss, where I ended up on her behalf, she has dragged me down even lower. She is the lightning rod for everything bad in my life. Forgiveness should not be wasted on such a woman. If I forgave her, I would be encouraging decent men and women to switch sides from light to darkness."

"You mentioned light. You loved your wife at some point and probably still do love her in your own way, so do not shut off that light. She is somebody's child. She is somebody's mom. Let her life be precious to you. Let her make it. Let her shine, even if she is shining on another man's mantle."

"Let her live so she can keep hurting decent, God-fearing men?"

"No, let her live so you do not join the ranks of men who've killed their wives in the mistaken belief that they had exclusive rights to those women and that if they could not have them, no other men could."

"My situation is different. I am in bankruptcy."

"That is your excuse. But you are proposing a vindictive, lethal solution to a human error, as sick men have been known to do. I don't believe you want to create a permanent problem for yourself and your kids, but you are seeking a justification for this action. That is an indication of evil. Malicious intent is evil in my wife's book."

"My mind is in a funk right now, but you need to hear my story. It is a true story.

"After I proposed marriage to this devil in Africa and returned here to file the necessary papers to bring her to the United States, my cousins discovered that she would never be allowed to enter because of her HIV status. I made a beeline back to Africa to break my engagement with her, and she admitted to me that she was HIV-positive."

"What? You knowingly got together with a carrier when you were not a carrier?"

"Yes, she admitted to me that she was a carrier but said that the problem was not at all related to promiscuity. She said witches had her infected with the virus after betting with her that she would never get a visa to the United States because she had turned down one of them who wanted to dillydally with her in her first year at the University of Nigeria. My cousins, knowing I am not interested in the debate over whether witches exist, countered her claim. They argued that witches had been known to do many things in our communities, but causing auto immune deficiency syndrome in virgin girls was not one of them.

Unfortunately, family members and friends could not get me to disentangle myself from this devil and her witchery. They asked my mom to help, and she came crying to my hotel suite. She tried to reason with me, saying that any marriage starting out with lies would not only have a short life span but would be injurious to whoever let the lies pass. In my arrogance, I ignored common sense and volunteered to play the role of hero to a wayward woman whom God in his infinite wisdom had designed as a punishment for an evil man. I stood by this woman and with the help of expensive smugglers finally brought her to this blessed country. See how she shows her appreciation? And you said something about forgiving?"

"Yes, I did say something about forgiveness. It was never designed to be awarded to perfect human beings, as my wife would say. It is meant to be given to the defective and worthless people in our lives."

"Sir," Emmanuel replied, "you are offensive to me. I hope you realize that and understand why I must take you down along with this woman. I know that those audio tapes you hear playing are in a foreign language—the one this woman, her lover, and I speak. Therefore, they mean nothing to you, but those are hours and hours of recordings of this woman discussing with her lover how and when to have me killed so she can take everything I own before going to be with him. She didn't simply want to leave me for another man. She wanted to destroy me first. Did I mention that because I have stood behind her despite her deadly disease, nobody in my family talks to me anymore? Why should they talk to someone whose judgment they no longer respect? I imported a woman carrying a deadly disease into God's country. I am worse than the sneaky serpent in Eden. That is the reason I am alone in the world. I am like Cain. I have become an abomination to all who see me. The temperature in hell cannot be cranked up high enough for my punishment."

"Guess what? This scenario is not unheard of in America. At least in movies and situation comedies, our mothers-in-law do not too much like us men. They are always putting us down by comparing us to the sons-in-law they never had. You do not see us killing our wives to even the score with their mothers, do you? You are a decent man. Act like one and hand me the gun along with the one in your waistband."

"Forget it, sir. I am not letting this woman walk. Because of this devilish woman, I am in financial ruin. So please allow me to be morally bankrupt as well. Allow me to shoot her. The bullet holes would serve as a warning to other women planning to use men as tickets, just as she used me to come to America."

"Hand over the guns, sir. Do it for the sake of your kids since it seems you can't do it for your own sake."

"You do not understand the resources it takes and the stress involved to bring a good, God-fearing woman from Africa to this land. To bring over an evil, manipulative woman, like the one here, costs infinitely more. Do you understand?"

"You're right. You can call me Mr. Ignoramus on that one. I have no idea what it takes to import a wife as you did. I have always liked my women big. America offered me a variety of them at a low cost or no cost at all. We do not do dowries here. So yeah, you're right. I don't have your experience. After all, I married an American woman when my army buddies were marrying slim model types they met overseas. But I know your investment has not been a total loss like the investments of some of your countrymen whom my wife knows."

"Just what do you mean by that when I told that I am in bankruptcy? I do not have a credit score anymore, thanks to her. Is there a worse hole to be in here than bankruptcy? Is there a deeper abyss in this land of personal freedom?"

"Yes, there are several holes worse than the one we call chapter 11 or bankruptcy, but since you have no experience with prison life, let's just say that not only are you still in the game of life but that you remain ahead. For starters, you have two beautiful babies to show for your investment. You should give thanks for them. Not having a credit score is not the same as having a bad credit. Just stay out of debt.

"My wife and I have had so much interaction with Africans that we are practically your historians. Some of your countrymen have fared worse than you in the area of wife importation. They received no consolation prizes after their investments tanked. Some are in prison for doing what you are trying to do. Some have died from high blood pressure and the stress of trying their hands at revenge. After all was said and done, they had nothing. Worst of all, they had no relationships with the kids they had with their American wives because they had emotionally abandoned them to pursue relationships with African babes they had barely known but had put on layaway anyway. Unlike you, those guys did not have the chance to make babies with their imported wives, because those girls jettisoned them at US entry ports by going home with other men."

"I will gladly accept rejection from any woman over bankruptcy," Emmanuel said. "In America, credit worthiness is everything. It is even more important than cash, which is supposed to be king. None of the men you are comparing with me has lost as much as I have by being in bankruptcy in the United States. My losses and suffering trump theirs."

"You may be very wrong about that. You know how in your culture very old men marry very young girls, girls who could be mistaken for their daughters? Well, I have a true story for you. Three men from the eastern part of your country went home and selected for themselves three girls from the elite federal government prep school, which I understand is a high school for kids whose politician daddies cannot afford schools in England. The men took responsibility for the education of those children. They gave the parents of those girls money to pay for tuition, room, and board. The men's sponsorship lasted through the next level of education: university. Those girls were the envy not just of other students but of the faculty. Because of their weekly receipt of dollars in the mail, the trio lived better than the queen of Sheba. But on getting over here, the girls blamed their parents for pairing them with men who had no fashion sense, men who still dressed in polyester, which was popular in the '70s."

"Obviously, the men were to blame for being conned."

"Not entirely, but notice that those were home-trained girls, in your parlance. Those girls were raised in Sunday schools in a culture steeped in respect for elders. They were imbued with high moral standards, obedience to elders, and respect for themselves and others. The pertinent question is why would such well-grounded girls leave designated betrotheds high and dry on getting to America? I could be wrong about this, but the fact that these girls kicked their parents' choices for life partners to the curb may be a symptom and not the cause of the problem men like you are facing."

"What are you saying? Is there an undercurrent that we are not aware of?"

"Are you sure you want to hear the real answer, the truth as opposed to PR and sympathy?"

"Your stories are a delaying tactic. However, they are not going to keep this devil from dying. But make the choice to live to tell your tales to other African men. You might help them to preserve their money and their sanity by convincing them not to go to Africa to marry over-glorified women."

"With your sense of entitlement, I do not know if you realize this. Most of you educated Africans act like you are Kuwaiti or Saudi royals. You can't abide having your authority questioned by underlings."

"No, we are not like those people," Emmanuel replied. "We let our women drive. We encourage them to focus on their education, building single-gender schools for them. When we need to marry extra wives, we do not just show up in our compounds with our latest acquisitions. We consult with our old wives before the new wives move in with us. We respect our women. It is therefore wrong, not just unfair, for you to bundle us up with a culture in which women are property."

"All I am saying is that maybe your young women are trying to send you a message that they did not appreciate the ways their moms were treated by their dads and other male members of their families. But you are high up on your thrones, too busy counting and branding your concubines to hear their complaints. That would explain why morally upstanding young ladies like the three I just mentioned, on getting to the land of the free, defy their parents at the risk of being disowned and pay you back in the only currency they know will get your undivided attention: revenge. Since you are not the first and won't be the last African man to receive this payback, do not harm the mother of your children. Taking a life is a very serious matter. Let the mother of your children live, okay?"

"Sir, you do not know the amount of money I have lost on account of this Jezebel. The Pell grants and other student loans I received would have been enough for me to build a mansion, complete with servants, for my widowed mother back in my village."

"I am sorry if you feel that I take your predicament lightly, but you should count your blessings. In so doing, you will stop the self-pity, which provides you with cover to do a serious evil with little thought. As that African party anthem of the disco era said, 'Carry your load and stop complaining.' After all, your situation may have something to do with what you did in the immediate past. For instance, did you marry a girl to regularize your papers, deliberately set her up to fail as a wife, quickly ferret out her faults, and leave her with kids so you could marry what you call a submissive African woman?"

"Sir, don't you think that question is a little bit intrusive and personal?"

"It is, but that is the nature of truth. It hurts. However, when you know the truth, it will set you free."

"Okay, you need to get out of my way now. The game is up."

"No, sir. Let me finish my thought first. My wife would say that there is a natural principle at work here. How we have lived our lives in the immediate past and how we conduct our lives presently determine what will happen to us in the immediate future. If you exploit, you will be exploited. But when heaven allows us to reap what we had forgotten we had sown, that does not mean heaven hates us."

"It does not?"

"It does not. But exploiters have short memories as you can testify. They forget what they do to others but keep accurate track of what others do to them. That's why you don't seem to have noticed that your country supplies professional exploiters to the rest of the world. Ask around and attend the lavish parties of other African tribes, and you will hear unbelievable stories. My wife has worked alongside many Africans in hospitals and nursing homes. She went to high school and college with some of y'all. She has also taught Africans. She reports that in the medical profession, the divorce rate is almost 100 percent among women who went to Africa to choose men and imported them as husbands to America. Almost all African nurses who did that lost the men they imported. Are you aware of that statistic? This is not a criticism, but you people exploit with impunity.

"The hypocrisy is that when it is your turn to be exploited, you want to impeach God for not playing divine sentry and keeping you safe from exploitative women. To me, the curious thing is that the women who lost out in those deals never considered killing their husbands as you are contemplating doing to your wife. Why are your women not planning to eliminate the men who have caused them to lose not just their investments but an important intangible?"

"What is that important intangible?"

"That would be time! Your women have lost time in addition to their investments. That is an intangible they cannot regain. I bet you the young men of your wife's age do not consider her matrimonial material anymore, do they? But you can run back to your country right now and find some girl in high school, and her parents would authorize you to take her as your bride. In fact, her parents, who would be closer in age than you are to her age, would be very glad to have you as a son-in-law simply because you live in America."

"That is the culture. Am I to blame for that?"

"Yes, sir. My wife says that any man who knows the right thing to do but refuses to do it is guilty of evil. You do know that though women generally live longer than men, they have a short shelf life as far as marriage and child-bearing are concerned. So why are you not playing fair?"

"You, sir, are defending people who need no defending. Those women you are rooting for are the so-called professional women who think that with their registered nursing licenses—which they consider a higher educational achievement than master's degrees and PhDs in applied physics, neuroscience, and genetic engineering—they own the world. But it is their fault that they have played the field so hard and sold themselves so short that they must rely on miracles to manufacture husbands. They can't find mates in America because African men willing to be walked on by their wives are in short supply, so these professional women must resort to recruiting husbands from home. They have cornered the market on men who are called professional applicants. Many years after college, these luckless men are stuck in low-paying jobs, denied advancement by their bosses, and are looking to escape.

"Those are the men the so-called professional women can control. Because of the earning potential of a registered nurse degree that America has provided, these women feel that the world is their oyster. They forget an Ibibio adage that says no one should be so good at diving into a river that he forgets to learn how to swim out of it. The women you are crusading for did just that. Consequently, in their arrogance, they raised the bar too high and waited so long for Mr. Right to show up that the marriage market adjourned on them. In merchandising that is called a shelf-life problem. You can't blame me and my fellow suffering African men for that."

"Are you sure that the so-called professional women are causing it to rain on their own parades?"

"Of course I am only a hundred percent sure. Without exception, all the African nurses you see strutting about in humongous sport utility vehicles, like Nebuchadnezzar looking down on the world from King Solomon's golden throne, were brought to this country not by their dads but through a visa program called 'wife joining husband.' Men borrowed money with extremely high interest rates from just about every loan shark and title-company they could find to show the American embassy that when the layaway women got to America they would not be a burden to US taxpayers.

"But upon reaching the United States and getting closer to making the big bucks, the men who rescued those evil women from abject poverty in Africa quickly became not just persona non grata in their own houses but doormats, things to be stepped on by the women they had suffered untold hardship to bring to America."

"The fact that you African men, as the comedian Rodney Dangerfield used to say, get no respect from your layaways denotes nothing personal. Blame it on the transformative power of money, particularly the American dollar. Money is an intoxicant. It is like power. It is a dangerous weapon in the hands of people suddenly inundated with it. I used to think that the lack of money made people do crazy stuff. But I was wrong. Sudden wealth, or too much money, distorts reality. It makes people feel that they run the world. Your women are no exception.

"My wife once used her connections to find me a high-paying job in the oil fields. I met a lot of people who had a lot of money at a very young age. There was a hard-working kid named Moore Richard who started to work in the oil business at age sixteen. During the boom years, he had built his parents a house in his native land. Over here, he bought himself a twenty-acre property, which he named Rich Ranch. He had a robust bank account and an expensive motorcycle and a seventy-thousand-dollar automobile in his garage. In the oil fields, company men, usually older white men, are treated like gods. Each day they make the kind of money regular oil-field workers make in two weeks during boom times. One day, Moore felt that a company man had said something disrespectful to him and to his tech, so he slapped the man and walked off the location. Today, even if he is asking only nine dollars an hour for job that pays $19.99, no one will hire him. No one will knowingly let him back on the oil field. So pride, which usually comes with sudden, unexpected wealth, does not permit more money to translate into more common sense for some people. Therefore, your women are not doing anything new under the sun."

"Women in Africa are not like that."

"They are. Women are the same all over the world. They want the good and easy life. They want equality. They want to be valued. They want to be respected. They want power. And they are quite capable of abusing that power just like men can."

"You are not an African. I am and I am telling you that women back home are not like this devil."

"That would explain why you left women in America and went thousands of miles to bring one back from Africa. How has that worked out for you so far?"

"Okay, rub it in. Thank you!"

"I am not rubbing it in. It is only that you do not examine yourselves. That is the reason it looks like that. There is one African in this city. You probably know him. So far, he has imported four wives. All of them have left him for other men within a year of getting here. He's probably working on another import as we speak. Albert Einstein was right in saying you should not do the same thing repeatedly and expect different results. If you do and your neighbors find out, there will be a lot of giggling and gossiping about your state of mind, if not mental health.

"I am saying that your angry, forceful insistence that your society not be allowed to keep pace with civilization is to blame for your losses. Your preference is that Africa not only remains paternalistic but should do everything to prevent women from being heard. That is the reason your married men run wild with loose women but demand to be obeyed and respected in the community. You pour encomiums on these men even if you know they are abusing their wives.

"On the other hand, if you failed to do your husbandly duties and meet your wife's needs and she decided to have a little fling with your driver, you would lean hard on the elders of your community to give you her head on a platter. Over here, we call that a double standard.

"You feel so entitled that you expect your wives to bow down, worship you, and refer to you as their lords and masters. You are so important in your own eyes while your wives are so insignificant. That is why after they are done taking care of the babies, washing and ironing your clothes, and cooking your food you sit on your behinds and insist that they serve you the food as well. You will not even get up to wash your hands at the kitchen sink. You expect your wives to bring you, your brothers, and other male family members water to wash your hands while you sit at table."

"Okay, what is wrong with that? Women are supposed to do these things. We do not train our women to become good moms only. They have to be good wives too. They know their responsibilities from a very young age."

"'Supposed' by whom? Your courts, which are always presided over by men? Where does it say in your constitution that the hand should wash the back but that the back need not wash the hand in return?"

"Do not blame us if you have negligently permitted your women to abdicate their responsibility to provide these services to you."

"I see. Like the husband of one of the new arrivals from Africa, you are clueless about how the Number One and leading nation in the modern world functions. My wife said the man I told you about won free visas to come here. I guess by your crooked standard, he should have gotten himself a brand-new trophy wife and brought her with him to America. But he did his wife what he considered a big favor. He brought her and their three kids to America. His wife is now pregnant with a fourth child. Your brother is not willing to work any job except in IT."

"You do not expect a highly educated Nigerian to come here and start flipping hamburgers like a high school dropout, do you?"

"Which begs the question, why do men from your class, the highly educated, crème de la crème of your nation, lie and cheat to come here when you could have stayed home and become captains of your industries and secretaries of the treasury? But that is a question for another time and for another audience.

"For now, let us agree that in a home with little people in diapers, it is irresponsible for the head of that household to be choosy about what job he accepts. Americans are a process-oriented people. Your brother is clueless about that. After dropping off the kids at day care and the wife at her job, pretending to look for jobs in his field, he spends the whole day at African food stores, talking about politics in the motherland, the same motherland he could not wait to escape.

"Meanwhile, after she gets off from her nurse aide job, he expects her to immediately go home, stand over a hot stove, and make him his favorite African food, foo-foo, because he does not eat American food."

"You're blaming the man for insisting on being fed the healthy, nonfattening, cholesterol-lowering, and preservative-free foods he grew up eating? For your information, African foods are very good for you. You should try some."

"I am not a dietitian, and I am not going to pretend that I'm dieting, so I am not going to get pinned down in that mine field. And besides, numerous studies have shown that despite where people end up on the economic ladder, they always prefer the foods they grew up eating and the music they grew up listening to. I am okay with that, but why should your wives not get a break? You want to eat traditional African food while living in America? Fix it yourself. Your wives have their hands full. They nurture the babies because, according to you, that is women's job. They go to school and they hold down two jobs. Why are these women also expected to cook after getting home, running from pillar to post all day? Meanwhile, their men have been watching soccer all day on the sixty-six-inch, 3-D, flat-screen television the wives worked overtime to pay for. I am sorry, but you are a cruel and sorry bunch."

"For your information, I bought my own flat-screen TV long before this evil camel moved into my space, so make an exception. This woman does not have the qualities of the African women your wife praises. There is no redeeming value in her."

"There is no human being like that. Every woman has something good in her."

"Not this one. No matter how deep and how long you excavate, you will never uncover a good aspect to a thoroughly evil woman like this one. She is evil through and through and proud of it. If she went back home, her parents would not be able to deal with the shame she has brought them. At the very least, they would commit her to a mental asylum so they could show their faces again in public."

"Why, because her marriage, like so many in America, ended before the loans taken to make the marriage happen could be paid off? The only people to whom marriage dissolution is not a function of living in America are first-generation Mmong people brought here during Cambodia's dark days and the Burmese brought here when their military was killing citizens like ants. But just wait till the descendants of these people come of age here.

"It would be nice if all American men would stay married to their women until the children they made together could finish college. But divorce, like other evils, will happen in our lives if we live long enough. We have to make room for it. I am sorry, but life goes on. It does not have to be cut short in order to avoid a divorce."

"Despite your extensive association with Africans of various tribes and stripes, you do not know our people as this devil and I do," Emmanuel said. "Our women stay in marriage for better or for worse. There is no wiggle room. The standard is absolute just like that injunction about children obeying their parents. The commandment does not allow you to treat your parents like dirt, no matter their economic or social standing. It is the same with marriage. It involves communities, not just you and a girl, and therefore she is not allowed to treat it like a trampoline, something to bounce in and out of at will."

"What about your men? They just go out and acquire new wives when the wives at home are no longer sufficiently young, obedient, sexy and hot, right?"

"No, when we marry new wives, we are doing the old ones a favor. We are providing them relief."

"Come on."

"Yes, that is the truth."

"I do not know what is in the water where you come from. I cannot identify the source of your chauvinism. Therefore, I'm not competent to rule that what warriors like you are doing to survive on the other side of the world is patently wrong. What I am saying is that since you were not brought here against your will as our ancestors were, you should do the polite, ethical, and American thing. Do not fight what has worked for us. If you are spoiling for a fight, go back home to the people who sent you here with the expectation that you would make something out of yourselves. There is no territory for you to conquer over here."

"We are not trying to remake America in our own image," Emmanuel said. "All we are asking is for you to stop interfering. America interferes in our marriages by giving our women too much freedom. That produces family problems and burdens your social welfare system."

"That is a small price to pay for freedom," David said. "The American goal is to extend freedom to all, particularly those within its boundaries. That offends you? Go home. Otherwise your condescension will pit you directly against our laws. If you chose not to adapt to America, please go back Africa.

"In America, our women have a God-given right to say no even to their husbands, not to mention their boyfriends. I have read so many news reports showing that you guys don't understand that. Africans have confused America laws with scarecrows. If you give me those guns and let your wife go, I will show you news stories about your fellow Africans, those not born here, who have become willing victims of our legal system."

"Did you say willing victims?" Emmanuel asked.

"Yes, I did. One of them was Atlas Akaiya, a very intelligent rich kid. He came here in March to attend engineering school so he could return and head his family business of running government-owned oil fields. In the summer, he took a geology class. Some students struggled with the fast pace and asked Akaiya for help. One of them was a young American female. One day, that girl also asked him for a ride. He obliged. On the way, they stopped at a restaurant to grab something to eat. After that, Akaiya suggested that they go to his apartment to do their homework. Once there they did more than just homework. Afterward, the girl calmly took a shower. She asked him to take her home since it was too late for them to see a movie as they had planned.

The next day the girl reported to the police that the consensual sex they had was not entirely consensual. The police did not buy that. They pointed out to her all the opportunities she had to back out of the situation. She told them that although she was three inches taller and about fifty pounds heavier than the guy, she was afraid that if she said no to his aggressive advances, he might have become incensed or violent and caused her harm, perhaps taking her life. Because of her fear, which she admitted she did not express to Akaiya, the jury found for her.

"I do not care about the laws of your country. Our laws mean business. They are not scarecrows designed to frighten away only small birds but to give a pass to the big and colorful ones. The laws on our books are no respecters of persons.

"That intelligent, promising young man is serving eighteen years in a Texas prison for not knowing when a no answer is implied or looking him straight in the face. After he's done his time, he will be deported back to your country without an engineering degree and with no prospect of becoming minister of petroleum. What a waste!

"Here is another story. It has to do with a damsel who, in the West Texas parlance of the Permian Basin, would be called a 'mighty fine young filly.' She was not lacking male attention. Visibly upset, the young woman told police that a coworker from Africa forced himself on her despite her protests. For that little fling, the state of Texas provided him with free food, clothing, and boarding in exchange for a major slice of his young life. Do you see a pattern here? A little fling can get you big time."

"Yes, I do, but whatever you think of me, I am not crazy."

"Then show the world that you love and value your freedom. Free your wife and free yourself. Put the gun down."

"The answer is no. I am a good man. This devil is not a good woman, and so she can't appreciate me. Despite her claim, I never enslaved her. I have never laid a hand on her. I have lived long enough in this state to know that hitting a woman is not just wrong but big trouble. I do not know the African men your wife has been tracking. This woman has lived in my house as if she were a guest. Nothing gets done here unless I do it myself. But since I heard a recording of this devil and her lover discussing plans to eliminate me, though have I continued to pay for the groceries, I have refrained from eating the entrées she has prepared. No cyanide-laced food for me.

"As for the IT guy your wife is spying on, I applaud him for insisting on maintaining his African identity and tradition as the head of his household, despite his economic situation in a land that is violently anti-tradition. His wife knows her place and what she is doing. May blessings be on her head for being her husband's crown jewel! Do not look down on her as a curiosity from prehistoric times. Unlike this devil here, she knows that one day she will return home, where people are never confused about gender, a place where gender roles are distinct."

"Correction, sir. Your women are jumping through hoops for you, fulfilling what your countryman and my wife's friend Elijah calls unrealistic expectations, because that is what they saw their moms do to put roofs over the heads of their children. Your mothers had no choice. Your fathers exercised iron rule over their wives, and tolerated no opposition. You grew up over there, so you know that dads had financial dominance over moms. These young ladies noticed the servitude you saw. Men like you accepted the situation because you were being readied to take over from your dads. The girls silently sided with their moms, whose plight had a special place in their hearts. They decided that one day and at some place they would do something about it. This is that day. And America is that place. This is the land of rights. The goal post has been shifted in favor of the previously powerless. The nursing profession has also given an advantage to your women. So when your wives arrive here, you get bad news.

"Because you are stubborn and entitled, instead of negotiating with them, you try to put a lien on them. As soon as they are able, they find loopholes, and those are plentiful in America. At work, at play, while shopping, and at school, they encounter American women whose moms never knew servitude and who have an acute sense of justice and fair play. After listening to your women's sad songs and concluding that your demands on your wives constitute cruel and unusual punishment, those Americans educate your scared-stiff women on what they owe themselves. And that lesson is usually quickly learned. That is the reason your hitherto docile, housebroken wives, after just a few hours in the United States, insist on being treated with the fairness, love, respect, and compassion that their moms back home never knew existed, let alone experienced.

"You and your cohorts, meanwhile, loudly make the false claim that your manhood has been irreversibly undermined by the Great Satan, America. But in this land of the brave and the free, the genie can't be put back in the bottle. Come to terms with that and be freed."

"Excuse me, sir. Please adjust your reading glasses so you can see clearly. Everything in this house belongs to me. This woman has never bought anything in this house, not even food. Despite what it cost to bring her to this country, I paid for her to go to nursing school. I have never seen a penny of her money and have never asked her how much she makes. Let me tell you what she has been doing with her money since she has been here. I pretended not to know, but I have a recording of her telling her lover that she would never let me touch her money. Therefore, when she gets paid, she converts the whole check into a money order or a cashier's check made out in her name and deposits it in a special account at the bank. I work so I do not bother. I am the victim here. You are not a victim of her crimes against me but strongly believe she is innocent. Since I am guilty in your book, you might as well let me avenge myself. When we stand before the Almighty, who he is reputed to be a righteous-judge and knows not just our actions but our intentions, he will decide which of us wronged the other more and deserves the lion's share of the punishment."

"Your wife is a victim of your tradition."

"She is bigger victimizer than a victim. Why are you blaming me?"

"You are angling for sympathy. That's why. In America, we may do drugs, in my own case, lots of them, but we definitely do not do sympathy. The American perspective, whether it has to do with laws, the economy, or taxes, has no room for sympathy. I have listened to your story of how you have been grossly wronged. Maybe you have repeated that story to yourself and to the thousands of your countrymen in this city and others, and since misery loves company, they sympathized and agreed that you have been gravely wronged. They may see redemption in killing your wife. That is your amen corner, but these people do not reflect reality as it relates to the law of this land. In your court system men with money are always found innocent even of heinous crimes against women. No matter what your men do to their wives, even the parents of the women will side with their sons-in-law and say that a whip is good for the back of a fool.

"You will have no such luck here. In Texas, if you shoot your wife or your girlfriend, even an overworked, court-appointed lawyer burdened with child-support payments will not ask a jury to sympathize with you because you were overcome by emotion after catching your wife doing another man in your house. Even if it were made up entirely of men from your church, a jury will not sympathize and equate the loss of a life with your loss of affection. It will sentence you to death.

"That sentence would mostly be for your foolishness in failing to realize that in Texas, there are more women than men. Therefore, there should arise no need for any man to kill a woman who, following the law of natural selection, decided to trade your love for that of a guy with more disposable income and newer, faster cars. Texas juries are generally pissed off at any man dumb enough to kill one fast, unfaithful woman and to deny himself the many opportunities to meet and go out with prayerful and potentially faithful women who dutifully fill the pews at singles-ministry services at evangelical churches twice weekly.

"Even the US government which has not yet reenergized its death penalty statute has a stake in this. It views it as a major wrong when an American is murdered."

"Correction, this animal is a Nigerian, not an American. She can't vote for anybody here, so she won't be missed after I have eliminated her."

"It does not matter. This is America. Every life is precious. Unlike nations with repressive regimes, America guards every life. Each is precious and matters. You take a life, and our law uses a heat-seeking missile to find and terminate you.

"You had ensured that she'd be here legally. Now she is an important person. The federal government relies on her to work and to pay taxes and to contribute to Social

Security so that it can continue to support America's aged. If you kill her, you must answer to the government. Follow the admonition to shed no blood."

"The admonition is 'to shed no innocent blood,'" Emmanuel corrected. "The rodent kneeling before me is no way innocent. It is okay to shoot her dead. I am ruined because of her. How can she be innocent? She lied about being a virgin. She knew she was no virgin."

"You were not a virgin either, so it does not matter."

"Yes, it does."

"Okay, but in the meantime, let her go."

"No. You still do not understand."

"Yes, you hurt. There is no doubt about that. But here is what I'm saying. The level of your hurt does not matter. What matters is your calm, mature response to it. Killing your wife will not relieve your distress and debt burden. You would do much better if you negotiated a settlement with her. You cannot recoup your losses by taking her life. If anything, that will create a bigger and more expensive problem. You will not escape death row. The state of Texas will make sure of that. It has a perfect record in that area. At the very least, you will lose your freedom to travel home to see your dear mother.

"Besides, after you have killed, except in war, the rest of your days on earth will be lacking in peace. Blood is a powerful thing that way. That is the reason that from the beginning, no one has been permitted to shed it. William Shakespeare rightly said that he who murders sleep shall not sleep. The same can be said of blood. That is the reason murderers seldom have peaceful nights. The ones I met while doing time confessed that if they had to live their lives all over again, they would never take a life for any reason. Neither would I. No real man would want murder to appear anywhere in his life's résumé."

"That means you have never been truly hurt by a woman, particularly a woman with devilish willowy eyes like this one. No, you have never been hurt."

"You are correct, but I know someone who has been truly hurt over and over again. She is living proof that if you love something and it flies away from you, you do not have to smoke it dead if and when you find it again."

"Whom are we talking about?"

"I am talking about my long-suffering wife. She has had many opportunities to do me in. I used to steal money from her. I cheated with the women who worked for her. Eventually I caused her businesses to fail."

"No decent Texan with two or three gun licenses to his name would let any child of Eve do all that to him and live to talk about it."

"You are right. My wife is from a small parish in Louisiana where gun permits are not required as proofs of residency. But what I am trying to tell you is that when you see a relationship, particularly a marriage, succeed, it is not a function of the partners contributing 50 percent apiece and sitting back and resting on their oars. For a marriage to work, for it to avoid running into the numerous hidden stumbling blocks, someone must willingly do more than his or her 50 percent share. Were you doing more for your marriage than your wife?"

"Yes I was and I am still doing it. What about you? Are you still cheating on your wife?"

"No."

"That is where our situations differ. My wife has cheated on me ever since I rescued her from abject poverty, showed her the good life, married her, and gave her the best that life could offer by coming to America. Cheating on me and trying to kill me are the thanks I got for all I have done for her. I bet your wife has done nothing like that. Or has she?"

"I have been the problem. But though I no longer cheat on my wife, I take no credit for that. It has nothing to do with me. It has everything to do with her. She gives more than her fair share without being preachy about it, without demanding I reciprocate. Giving without ceasing is her modus operandi. If I hadn't been a full-time jerk, her exemplary character—and my reaction to your countrymen's behavior—could have transformed me into the decent husband a woman like her deserves far sooner."

"Have my countrymen ever done right by you?"

"Not on a regular basis. But they did certify that I've got a good woman. My woman is a naturally tolerant person. But take it from me, I have done more evil to my wife than your wife has ever done or will ever do to you. We drug users are like that. Our brains do not or cannot keep track of our actions. The demons on our backs do not allow for even the briefest introspection. That is the reason we do evil things to people, even the people we claim to care about, without realizing we are hurting them. You have never used drugs, so do not act like us users. It's not a badge of honor. I asked you to let your wife go. You've got to let her go, man."

"How can you keep asking me to do that after I have described the pain and wretchedness I have suffered at the hands of a traitor whom I have finally cornered? No sir, I am not letting her off. It is payback time. Today is her judgment day. Her executioner, that would be me, is ready. So stand back please."

"Hold on, please. Are you familiar with a tool called opportunity cost?"

"I am college-educated, remember?"

"Then I guess not. According to my wife, those of you in school during the wasted decades of military rule in your country had been heavily deprived. You attended school only some of the time, and you got no education. Unless you went to one of the schools, like the so-called government colleges of the federation, that members of the oligarchy set up to give their kids private-school experiences at government expense, your schools provided no real education, because at the behest of what was called military regimes, schools would be shut down for upward of nine months a year. My wife says that most of your medical doctors trained during military rule did not learn enough medicine and therefore cannot pass the American Medical Association test to practice in America.

"Such half-baked health care providers may be politically connected, but they are quacks. She said they would not be allowed to get close to a health care facility in America. But they are decision-makers in your country. They practice medicine over there, because no one is keeping track of patients who die at the hands of half-baked, utterly worthless physicians. I understand that no one is held responsible for deaths at health facilities, so I am not surprised that you do not see how the choice you are making in this situation could affect your freedom. Our laws will get you, though. They never fail to hold lawbreakers accountable."

"You make it sound like patients do not die at American hospitals, hospices, and care homes."

"It is very sad if that is the only thing you have taken from what I just told you."

"That is what I heard you say."

"Have you ever worked in the oil fields?"

"No, sir."

"Then let me see if I can illustrate this anyway. At the oil drilling locations, anything and everything can go wrong. Producers, exploration and production companies, operators, and oil-field services companies know that. The companies involved in the oil business have got lots of money, but they want to make more. Therefore, they are vigilant and take nothing for granted. You should not either. They hire company men and safety coordinators to make sure no worker is doing unsafe things that could cause injury or death and hurt the companies financially and in public opinions.

"At drill locations, you will also see trucks loaded with equipment idling for hours, if not days. Some of those vehicles carry electric generators, emergency showers, eye-wash stations, and emergency medical personnel who seem to sit around all day doing nothing. To the naked eye, it would appear that this is a waste and that the companies are polluting the environment by letting diesel-powered equipment run forever. But an astute economist would argue that since everything has a cost associated with it, the decisions you make and the actions you take always require careful thought. You must always be ready. Otherwise, you hurt your freedom and your pocketbook."

"You do not have to be an economist to know that. Everyone with a functioning brain knows that."

"That is not quite so. People are not born that way. Take you, for example. Cost-benefit analysis is a learned behavior. If people instinctively considered what their actions would cost before taking them, the prisons would be empty. They would look like church buildings in London, which have been reduced to tourist attractions."

"What about me?"

"You display what my wife calls 'learned ignorance.' With your high level of education, you are just like hundreds of confused America kids enticed by the expectation of effortless riches into drug-dealing while still in high school."

"That is cold."

"But that is the truth. I have talked to you so much and for so long that I'm winded. Still, I'm not making progress. You place no value on your freedom."

"I am a grown man who has suffered a great deal and has lost a great deal at the hands of one evil woman."

"You are a grown man quiet all right. However, that guarantees nothing as you demonstrate by your cavalier attitude toward your most valuable asset, your freedom. Like kids, you are acting as if you are made up mostly of adrenaline. Young people stand knee-deep in that hormone, which makes them do things without paying attention to what their actions might cost them. If you do not understand opportunity cost, you lean toward doing wrong for what you consider a right reason. Young drug dealers see the money to be made and the easy life to be had, not the potential curtailment of their freedom. You are a grown man. Again, what is your excuse for the ignorance you display?"

"I used to have a perfect credit score. Not only is that ruined, but now I'm in bankruptcy because of one evil woman."

"Let me tell you about African women who have been conned by your men but who have not wasted valuable time trying to kill those men. As a matter of fact, one girl tried to kill herself for what she considered her foolishness. It never occurred to her to kill the man who took from her all that she had.

"This is a true story. One of your people named Paul brought over a super-smart kid from Nigeria. She was his niece named Uduak-Abasi, which he said meant "the will of God." She preferred to be called Judy. Paul brought her here to attend pharmacy school and for no other reason. She was accepted into the elite pharmacy program at Southern Texas University. He paid all her expenses. After she obtained her pharmacy doctorate, Paul wanted her to head back home to run a county-government owned dispensary, as was the original plan. She refused and moved out of her uncle's house, where she had been living rent-free. She neither bothered to inform him nor offered a reason for moving out.

"One Sunday evening, Paul summoned other Africans to his house and tasked them with finding out from Judy what wrong he had done her. She told them she was grown and thus was ending the previous living arrangement. She did not want to live with Paul and his American family anymore. His people told the uncle that this being America, his niece had a right to do as she pleased.

"Paul later found out that Judy had bought a house in a lily-white suburb in New England. Much later, Paul's wife, who had a closer relationship with Judy than he did, discovered the reason for Judy's defiance. She informed Paul that Judy was shacking up with another African, a man she called Dr. Williams. Paul had money to burn, so he had the guy followed. The private eye found out that Judy's paramour was a follow Nigerian. He graduated from high school in the 1970s. During that period in Nigeria, questions and answers to the high school graduation test used to be sold on the open market.

At that time Williams was nicknamed Promoter because he made money from selling questions to the test even when he was in junior high. Much later in America, he was one of those Nigerians who claimed that they went to medical schools in Nigeria. They had the papers to back up their claims. The only problem was that these people could not pass the registered nursing test, let alone the unforgiving American Medical Board examination, which all newly minted physicians must clear to be called doctors. The private eye found out that Williams had just one attempt left before he was barred from taking the test again. He proposed marriage to Judy so she could work and pay the bills while he concentrated on the preparation for the medical board test

"Judy was beyond excited to be courted by the extremely good-looking Williams and said she would back his quest to attend medical school in what used to be called the West Indies. Paul heard about the marriage proposal and went to see Judy at the John Prichard drugstore, where he had used his connection to land her a job. She claimed she was too busy to visit with him. Paul felt insulted and quietly left the store. But instead of going home, he got Tony, a guy who worked at the photo lab at another John Prichard location. They went to see Judy. Paul asked the store manager for permission to talk to Judy in private, and he granted the request. Tony told Judy that the man she was shacking up with was a member of a syndicate that made money leaking high school graduation tests in Nigeria. Judy responded that mistakes of youth should never be held against a person in adulthood.

"Tony responded that besides what she considered a youthful indiscretion, her fiancé had a habit of taking pictures of his women in compromising positions without their knowledge and would bring in the film to be processed and the pictures sold. He said those actions clearly indicated a pattern of immorality. Judy accused Tony of fabrication. The man told her that he once recognized one of the women in the photos and confronted Williams. That confrontation led to an altercation in which her lover sustained a black eye. Paul challenged Judy to confront Williams with this information and see what he would say. Judy said she would not do that. He asked her if she was afraid to find out that he was peddling her nude pictures for profit or that she was dealing with a lying, untrustworthy, immoral man. Paul assured her that the proposal by Williams was a ruse and that their relationship would not progress beyond that.

"Judy walked out on her uncle, got on the intercom, and called security to the pharmacy. Before security arrived, Paul told her it was bad enough that Williams was getting her amenities, which include her gold stash, for free, but for him to use an insincere marriage proposal to prove that she was a perfect fool was beyond the pale. He reminded her that years back, after her sister Margaret had obtained a first-class honor's degree in system engineering and had landed a high-paying job with a French oil concern, a mild-mannered and an extremely good-looking gentleman had dangled a marriage proposal in front of her. She had taken the bait.

"That ruse kept Margaret from going to graduate school as her father, a high school principal, had planned. Two babies later, instead of the marriage she was promised, Margaret wound up missing under mysterious circumstances and was never found. This time, Paul said, he would fight the fake marriage proposal to his last breath.

"Paul did not know it then, but there would be no fight. Williams had already won in a knockout. He had Judy completely wrapped around his little finger.

"That weekend, Judy told her man about the 'absolute nonsense' her uncle's paid character assassin had tried to make her buy. Williams again pledged his undying love to her. He told her that their wedding would be held at the Calabar sports stadium, a showpiece that Judy's state chief executive, General U. J. Esuene, had just built for the people. After this assurance from the man she always described as a doctor working on a cure for all cancers, Judy put her new house on the market. She changed all her phone numbers and her job. She moved to a gated community more exclusive than the one she had just left. Thus she cut herself off not just from her uncle and his wife Brenda but from everyone else except for a couple of pharmacy technicians she was mentoring.

"Though her man had no job, Judy put his name on all the paperwork for the new house but paid the mortgage by herself. She also paid for all the expenses at the mansion.

"Judy took a second job as an adjunct professor at her alma mater to make more money so she could pay for the upcoming society wedding back home in the holy city of Calabar, Nigeria. With approval from Williams, she sent home a forty-foot shipping container with all her wedding stuff. Shortly after that shipment reached Nigeria, Williams's mother came to visit. Judy was proud to show her off as her mother-in-law. She took her to a beauty shop weekly and had the woman's hair dyed, relaxed, permutated, and the grays tinted. They went shopping whenever Judy got home from work. She took her on walks in the parks and around Braes Bayou. To keep her from feeling lonesome in the house, Judy introduced her future mother-in-law to daytime TV and to the *Oprah Winfrey Show*.

"One day, Paul received calls from a couple of Judy's pharmacy-technicians saying she had neither been seen nor heard from for two days. Paul told them he had no information about her. They gave him her address and begged him not to say how he got it. They insisted he should check on her immediately. Paul detoured from where he was heading, got to Judy's house in the twinkle of an eye, and called the police, who forced open the door. The police found Judy with no pulse and called an ambulance.

Apparently, Williams's mom had gone back to Africa after three months in the United States. Judy had outdone herself by organizing a huge send-off party for the woman she called *Mamami*, or "my own mother."

One day, Judy had rushed back from work to wait for the arborist she had hired to prune some boughs. The president of her neighborhood association had sent a letter saying that a bough on a tree in Judy's front yard was illegally hanging over the sidewalk, threatening to brush joggers and walkers as they passed by her house. The legal document warned that since the infraction could lower property values in the high-priced subdivision, if Judy did not correct the problem in two days, the association, backed by bylaws and city ordinances, would send its own landscaping crew to correct the situation. That operation, the letter said, would cost Judy $2,500, which would be billed in two installments. Judy did not know anyone who had won a fight with a homeowners' association, so she decided to comply. That was the reason she skipped some of the overtime hours she was scheduled to work and went home early. She parked her vehicle on the street instead of the driveway and went to the front door to get her mail. Judy noticed several letters from her bank, indicating she did not have enough liquidity to cover her cable, light, and other regular bills. She knew the bank had made a mistake and made a mental note to call in the morning. She went upstairs.

"After a quick shower, she got dressed and went to the front door to see if the tree guy was on the driveway waiting for her. He was not and did not answer his phone. After waiting for what seemed like an eternity, Judy walked under the trees to see what she was up against. She went to the kitchen to grab a knife. It looked to her like she could do the trimming herself with a steak knife. While she was selecting a knife, she heard a familiar voice behind her and almost jumped out of her skin.

"Mama had returned. While Judy was trying to express her surprise at the sudden and unannounced return of her dear mama and to apologize for her carelessness in not realizing that someone else was in the house, a homely young woman emerged from behind Mama.

"Mama pushed the pimple-faced youngster in front of Judy and began to cry big blobs of tears. She apologized to Judy, begging her to understand and to forgive Emeka for the 'sins of his people.'

"'What are you talking about, Mamami?' Judy asked.

"Mama explained that after she returned home, everybody was pleased to see her appearing so healthy and asked for her secret to looking even younger than the women who had gotten married decades after she had. She said she told them an excellent cook of *edikang-ikong* soup, a nice, well-educated, and rich woman her son was living with, had taken good care of her while she was in America. She told them her son had proposed marriage to the woman. But upon learning that Emeka's fiancée was not an Ogutal town woman, they were alarmed and reminded her that since, with his high-level of education, her son could become a king of the town and the county, he was not at liberty to marry outside the county. They were surprised that she, as a leader of the Ogutal Women's Progressive Union, was not responsible enough to remember the two things an Ogutal king was not allowed to do: make a trip that might entail him spending the night away from his domain and marrying an outsider, a non-Ogutal woman.

She told Judy that the elders and pillars of Ogutal demanded that she right the situation immediately. That was the reason she had to return to America so soon after she had left.

"Mama wrapped her hands around Judy and begged her not to blame Emeka for a turn of events over which he had no control. She swore to her that her son had no say in the culture of her people, particularly as it related to whom their probable king would marry. She praised Judy for being such a good girl. Mama assured her that given her beauty, wealth, and good nature, she would soon find another man who might be an even better fit for her than her son Emeka.

She said she knew and trusted in her heart that Judy would understand and let Emeka move on with his life and leave her mansion to be with 'the gal the village had chosen and sent to him.'

"Judy was numbed. She had almost finished a double shift at a busy pharmacy. Her mind could not process anything the woman gripping her shoulders was saying. She believed she was hallucinating from a lack of sleep. Then she heard the door open and slam shut. The noise reoriented her to the correct latitude and longitude. She looked up to see Mama walking out of the house with the girl. Judy noticed that they were not dressed for the wintry weather outside. She didn't know where the pair was heading, but she decided to give them a ride. She went upstairs to get her keys and a coat and opened the garage door. The white BMW she had bought for ninety thousand dollars was missing. She had planned to ship the car to Calabar that weekend. It was to be used to transport her and her bridesmaids to the wedding at Sacred Heart Cathedral. Still, she was not alarmed that the automobile was not there. Her only concern was that Mama might catch pneumonia. To prevent that, Judy jumped into her sport utility vehicle and drove to find Mama and to take her wherever she was going. Mama was no way in sight. From the subdivision, Judy drove to the Southwest Freeway, an interstate highway about a mile and a half away. Still no Mama in sight. That bothered Judy.

"In the Great Sherwood Forest subdivision where she lived, there was only one entrance and one exit. Buses did not run there. So Judy wondered how Mama could have vanished without a trace in broad daylight. She went to the security booth to inquire. The security officer told Judy that an expensive, white, German-made automobile had picked up two women just moments before she got there. Judy returned home and went upstairs to hang up her jacket in the master bedroom's walk-in closet. She discovered that the section belonging to her fiancé had essentially been swept clean. In a daze, she went downstairs to see what else was missing from the house. Judy looked in the living room, the dining room, and the hallways. All the photographs with Williams's images on them were gone.

"What did all this mean? Judy did not want to find out. All she knew was that life was no longer worth living if she was going to live it without her prince, the man she had trusted with all her earthly and spiritual possessions, the man who had told her that he would rather die a horrible death than live a day without his princess. Judy suddenly felt old, empty, an—worse—alone. She flew upstairs as if to escape the horror that had flooded the first floor of her house. She got into bed. Deciding that she wanted to die happy, Judy swallowed a mixture of colorful capsules and pain relievers and washed them down with top-of-the-line bourbon and well-aged whiskey, which she had planned to hand-deliver to Williams's dad, her proposed father-in-law."

"Did she die or not?" Emmanuel asked.

"No," David said. "The EMTs would not let Judy meet her maker quite so soon without making an appointment first. They summoned a helicopter, which transported her to an emergency room, where medical workers pumped out her stomach and forced her to stay in the land of the living and continue to deal with rush-hour traffic and to pay sales and property taxes like the rest of us."

"What did she do to Williams after being pulled from the jaws of death?"

"She did nothing."

"What do you mean she did nothing to him?"

"That is what I am trying to tell you. In the game of life, we sometimes win by losing."

"How did you arrive at such an unnatural, defeatist conclusion?"

"Actually, that is not my conclusion. I am much like you. I do not let go. I do not forgive. I believe strongly in an eye—and maybe two eyes, a nose, and an ear—for an eye. But my wife says that Judy wound up winning big."

"What? Are saying that before Judy had the chance to blow out his brains, the self-described Dr. Williams died of an early heart attack, and she became the beneficiary of his half-million-dollar life insurance policy?"

"No, she had no interest in a windfall like that. Suffice it to say that she has had a fulfilling life after going to hell and back."

"What happened? Did she become a nun?"

"In a way, she chose the cloistered life. She became a celibate for a time but not in the way you think. After she was released from the hospital, other Nigerian men, like sharks smelling blood in the water, wanted a piece of her too. To keep her from being used and abused again, Uncle Paul forcibly moved her about 355 miles down Interstate 45. That exile was good for her. She found a fellow pharmacist she nicknamed the Will of God. After a short courtship, she introduced him to her uncle. Paul had his doubts, but knowing that Judy was one of those women who believe every woman should have a man, he did not stand in her way. He informed the people at home that Judy had found a good man to marry. Together Judy and Pius Samuelson Johnson started a business, the profits from which have been poured into her passion, the African Medical Project, which provides medicine, shoes, and school uniforms to orphans in the rural area of her state and beyond. As that play-by-play sports commentator used to say on radio after his team won, 'How sweet it is!'"

"Today Dr. Williams is serving twenty-five years at a federal prison in Beaumont, Texas, for defrauding the US government."